FALLING FOR GRACE

FALLING FOR GRACE

AN ANTHOLOGY OF AUSTRALIAN LESBIAN FICTION

EDITORS - ROBERTA SNOW - JILL TAYLOR

BlackWattle Press
Sydney Australia
1993

Some of the stories included here have appeared, in whole or in part, in *Australian Short Stories, Cargo, Hecate,* and *BURN. The Wound & the Message* by Mary Fallon is extracted from *Working Hot,* Sybylla Co-operative Press. *The Lobster Queen* and *The Frilling Machine* by Susan Hampton is from *Surly Girls,* Collins Imprint. *A Small Story* by Pamela Brown is from *Keep It Quiet,* Sea Cruise Books. Excerpts in *Falling for Grace* are from *Treachery at St Monica's* by Iërne Ormsby, Hutchinson's Girls Annual, Hutchinson & Co (Publishers) Ltd 1938

Publication of this title was assisted by the Australia Council, the Federal Government's arts funding and advisory body.

Published by BlackWattle Press
PO Box 4, Leichhardt, NSW Australia 2040
July 1993

© 1993 Cover Art by Kaye Schumack, High Line Design

Printed by Southwood Press, Marrickville NSW

ISBN 1 875243 12 7

WOMENCRAFTS, INC.

376 Commercial Street
PROVINCETOWN, MA 02657
(508) 487-2501

SOLD BY		DATE	
NAME			
ADDRESS			
CASH	C.O.D.	CHARGE	ON ACCT.
			795
			+40
			835

Deposits Non-Refundable

RECEIVED BY
Thank You For Your Matronage

35294   *Thank You*

All claims and returned goods MUST be accompanied by this bill.

Thank You WE APPRECIATE YOUR BUSINESS

Fill out in duplicate with one copy for customer. Simply insert a carbon between the sheets — or fill out each copy separately

PROMISSORY NOTE

$ _____ Date _____ 19 _____

For Value
Received, I, _____

Promise to pay to the order of _____

_____

the sum of _____

to be paid as follows: _____

_____

_____

with interest to be paid, at the rate of _____
per centum per annum, from date payment is due.

_____ L.S.

_____
(FOR SIGNATURE OF CUSTOMER)

SIGNED AND SEALED IN PRESENCE OF:

_____
(WITNESS)

NEBS, Inc. Groton Mass. 01471. To ORDER PHONE TOLL FREE 1 + 800 225 6380

Contents

Foreword

Hello Patients...

As a psycho sexual therapist with twenty years experience in grappling with the enormous pool of unmet libidinous need in the lesbian community, it is with an informed sense of urgency that I exhort you to read this book very carefully.

Why is it imperative that you read this book? There are so many reasons. This lively volume rips back the veil of secrecy and silence that has historically obscured the shadowy twilight underworld of the female invert. The 'love which dare not speak its name' has of course been chattering uncontrollably for centuries. But all too often the canon of published lesbian scribblings has been characterised by a discouraging mix of euphemism and suicidal depression.

In this volume, the girls have got their hands on a few publishing dollars and we hear the more confident and frank voice of the 1990s.

It's a voice I hear all the time from my invert patients at my lucrative chain of private clinics. Every morning, before the clinic doors open, you see the girls with very short hair, very big leather coats and very stroppy dogs, queuing up to see me. They come into my rooms, loosen their clothing, lie down on my couch and they tell me their frank stories. Stories of lesbian love and lust in the latter half of the twentieth century. Stories just like the stories that follow in these pages.

Stories of the 'dangerous tenderness' one woman can feel for another as she looks at 'softly tanned shoulders cut by the line of a pale blue singlet'. Stories of the inchoate longing that troubles and stirs the core of so many female friendships, as women instinctively reach for each other within the very shadow of husbands and convention. Stories of 'stray lust' at an office party and of violent rage at the brutal prejudice, often whispered in ignorance, that lacerates the heart.

Feminism may have destroyed that part of the female brain which controls spelling, but the 'wimmin' writers on these pages have the confidence to grasp and revitalise the ancient tradition of Sappho. Their sexual love for each other is confidently expressed, whether in the 'carpet-lined smoke boxes' of an urban bar, or in the very bosom of the family at an Aussie wedding, where the bridesmaid has her eye on the bride.

Why do these modern lassies still need to come to my clinics? It's not to grapple with accepting their sexuality I can assure you of that. The inverts of the '90s are so 'hot to trot' (to use a medical term) their psycho sexual problems arise from a surfeit of pleasure, an excess of opportunity, or to put it plainly, 'too many lollies in the lolly shop', or 'too much nooky with too many gals'. It's the plethora of choice that confuses modern girls. Once you've read this book, you'll see what I mean. I commend these stories to you and look forward to seeing you at one of my clinics.

Dr Mary Hartman
(Appointments can be made by writing to her Matron, Julie McCrossin)

GINA SCHIEN

Minnie Gets Married

A N N   S A T in the back of the car next to little Deb and Katie. Her dress creaked. Her nasal passages were clogged with the perfume that weddings are drenched with. Or maybe it was some cheap stuff the twins had on. She breathed, quick and shallow, trying to clear her head.

"You right?" The chauffeur turned his head and little Deb and Katie looked at her.

"Yep. Sorry. Ha."

Little Deb looked up at her.

"Will there be food soon?"

"I hope so."

"Why are you so tall?"

"Why are you so nosy?"

"Just askin'."

The limousine purred on in silence. Ann examined her hands, which were nested in her lap, until the car stopped outside the RSL club. The driver stood at her window, opening the door, helping them out.

The three bridesmaids looked beautiful out in the sunlight. Mrs Bellini and Mr Bellini stood and smiled at the two little cuties (Stevie's kid sisters), with their little rings of flowers around their heads. That tall Ann, little Minnie's friend, was (it had to be said now that she was closer) actually looking the worst for wear after the service. Minnie's brother Peter peered into her face, concerned. His face was raw from shaving.

"You don't look so hot," he said.

"I don't feel it either." He put a hand on her shoulder.

"I'm amazed you did this."

"From this point on, I'm here for the alcohol."

Just as she was getting the hang of walking in those shoes over the grass Mrs Bellini scooped Ann's hand up and placed it gingerly in her own.

"Ann, in case I don't get to you later…"

Wait till I get to you, you little pervert!

"I just want to say thank you because we do appreciate it."

"That's fine, Mrs Bellini." Her hand was dropped.

And then the MC positioned them in a subdued V shape at the club door. Her and the two littlies; their tiny hands thrust into her own. "Stand

3

here till I call you."

He disappeared. Where was Minnie? They stood rustling in hot silk. Rooted to the spot, wavering uncertainly like three pulsating blue lilies.

"Bridesmaids, Ann and little Deb and Katie!"

The twins had to lead this huge lumbering woman, who clearly had no idea how to walk (how embarrassing for them) into an important event. Ann was expecting, hoping for, semi-darkness but it was incredibly, rudely, bright. There was the Bellini family. Her own seat was next to Minnie's tiny Aunt Luisa and her own partner Ian, who was Minnie's cousin. Aunt Luisa craned to kiss Ann on the cheek and patted her down like a wilful dog.

"Well, Annie, sit sit sit ..."

Even when she had sat obediently, Ann towered over the diners like a mournful crane among merry-making, chattering sparrows. Aunt Luisa poured her champagne.

"Yuk. Soup!" the twins said.

"And now can we please welcome ..." the MC boomed. "For the first time, Mr and Mrs Nikkaleiedes!"

Minnie and Steve swept into the room. Clear across the room, Ann could see the snail trail of tears down Minnie's cheeks.

My Minnie, my sweetie pie. Careful kid.

Aunt Luisa patted her hand. "They look wonderful, don't they?"

"One more kiss for the cameras," the MC boomed. It was an order.

Minnie stood with Steve at the door. Steve ran his hand over the back of his head again and again, as if wondering where all his hair had gone. There was a storm of flashes while Steve kissed Minnie, once, again, and again, on damp cheeks. "That enough?" he asked.

"The church kiss was longer," teased the MC. "And more on target." He was a devil! He'd always found that ignoring the tears was the best shot and so Minnie was led gently to a seat, a freshly crowned but bewildered princess. She was six places away from Ann.

The littlies ran up and down behind the tables for the rest of the courses, too excited to eat. The soup was good. Little Deb and Katie had stored their bowls under the table, but were playing a game with the croutons.

For one moment, or maybe two, Minnie caught Ann's eye and smiled. Ann raised an eyebrow and smiled back, showing what she hoped was an elegant irony, as if to say 'look at this hand that life has dealt us'. Then it was time for the telegrams. As in wartime, the arrival of a message could mean life or death.

"Could we have a bit of shoosh please." The awful MC handed over the mike to the best man. The hand that held the telegrams shook.

"To Steve, roses are red, violets are blue..." The mike was adjusted but the shaking hand couldn't be helped. "... if you don't get some tonight, then what good are you?"

Har Har! Steve's Dad was nodding in approval while a line of Bellini relatives pfffed and snorted into their hands and glasses.

"To Steve and Minnie, best wishes from Mr Fuggin, Mrs Fuggin and the whole Fuggin family."

Snort, pfff!

"Dear Steve and Minnie, best wishes from the class of '79."

So tame! Ann closed her eyes.

To dearest Minnie, I love and lust after you but I don't forgive you. I miss sex with you. What a team we were! Your loss, honey. Hot kisses from your bridesmaid, Annie.

"More champagne, Ann?"

"Thanks Aunt Luisa."

After the cake was cut, symbolising their first action taken together, Steve and Minnie danced the bridal waltz. The wedding party watched in polite silence. They shuffled back and forth. An unerringly flicked crouton from little Deb crunched beneath Minnie's heels.

Aunt Luisa felt that something was wrong. Her smile faded. She frowned. A sensitive radar seemed to emanate from her. Her head moved back and forth as though she were a psychic sniffing out the scent of the future. She gave a low questioning moan. She was tracking down a very clear signal.

"What's wrong, Aunt Luisa?"

Ann looked at Luisa just as the same thought occurred to both of them: Minnie would not end up with this man, this Stevie. And should not. Not at all! Aunt Luisa studied her plate, her dark brows knitted.

Ann smiled into her champagne. So all was not lost.

"Good food, eh." Ian, who was adjusting his bow tie, belched. "We're next." He drained his glass because this was going to be tough, dancing with this girl Ann.

"And the bridesmaid and partner, Ann and Ian!"

Ann nearly jerked him off his feet in her hurry to get to the floor and her little Minnie.

"Steady on!" Ian said. The girl was huge and gawky.

"And little DebnKatie!" The MC could have been calling raffle winners.

So now there were six of them in this circus. The little twins clutched each other, their flowers skew-whiff over their ears, and swayed in a parody of Steve and Minnie. Ian and Ann did a neat, precise lap of the floor. Dancers in a formal situation are bonded by the need to follow ritual. They depend upon each other not to betray the collective dignity. Differences are forgotten. Ian started to relax into the moment when they approached the happy couple for the second time.

"Minnie!" it was an urgent but restrained whisper that he could hear coming from right next to his head. Bloody Ann. Maybe she'd dropped something. He looked at the floor.

"Minnie Min!"

Shut up.

"No!"

Minnie was looking at Ann over Steve's shoulder. Ian tried to dance away from them but that made it worse. The next whisper was louder.

"Are you sure, Minnie?"

Minnie was whimpering, for God's sake.

"Are you!!"

MC had never seen anything like this string bean woman who was whirling her partner round like a dervish. She seemed to be hissing at the poor little bride.

"And now ladies and gentlemen. When you're ready to join these lovely couples, get up and have a spin!"

Ian was about to suggest sitting down, now that there were plenty of other couples up, thank Christ, when he felt Ann melt away from him. Ann tapped Steven on the shoulder.

"Excuse me. May I?" Quicker than a wink she scooped up Minnie, her little Min, around the waist. Steve and Ian stood and watched.

"For fuck's sake." But Steve was as nothing next to her. A mere speck.

She was dancing with his wife.

Steve looked at Ian.

"She's dancing with my wife, mate."

Ian nodded.

"Maybe that's what you're supposed to do. D'you wanna drink?"

Minnie tried to look at Ann but the overwhelming familiar smell of her, the feel of her body, was enough.

"Jesus, Ann. Jesus!"

"You signed my dance card, remember?"

The stringbean and the crowned princess swirled around the floor, scattering little Deb's croutons.

Minnie was half laughing, half groaning with embarrassment. Ann was in her stride, now that action had been taken. "Remember when we came home from that party? Remember we fell asleep on the lawn and your mother found us in the morning?"

"Is this supposed to make me feel wistful?"

"Yes. I want you to remember. Remember everything."

"Mum said we were perverted."

"No! She said I was perverted. You are still her baby daughter."

Other couples, looking and then looking again, were laughing. Peter waltzed past and winked.

"Did you set this up with Peter?"

"Certainly not! Could have done though."

Little Deb and Katie waltzed past professionally.

"When do we get cake?"

Minnie smiled at them. "Soon."

Little Deb watched them a bit more. "Why are youse dancing together? You shouldn't be dancing together."

"It's the tradition for women to dance together at weddings."

"Oh, sure."

"Anyway look at you two."

Ann turned back to Minnie.

"Remember when we danced together for the first time?"

"Whah yayes!"

Minnie and her southern accent! It was a good sign.

Inside herself, Ann crowed. Quick! More!

"Remember when your mother found us kissing in the garden?"

"Why did everything happen in the garden?"

"The smell of hot lawn and your gardenias. There was something… *labial* about them. To put it quite frankly they smelt of fanny."

"Please!"

"Yes Min, I'm afraid they brought out the butch in me."

"Not in that dress, mate."

"See what I do for you? I cross-dress for you. Would Steve do that? I'll even kiss you if you like."

"If we kiss, then this wedding is finishing. My marriage is a sham."

"Then I will, definitely."

Ann pressed her body closer to Minnie's and kissed her cheek. Mrs Bellini, her eyes narrowed, was watching from her seat.

"I love you."

"I love you."

"Even better. Marry me! I have a limousine waiting."

"My mother's looking a bit strange."

"Well, well, well. Are we surprised?"

Mrs Bellini was standing, walking, brushing away Peter's hand. Aunt Luisa watched her sister approach, then turned and watched the stringbean Annie with her little niece.

Mrs Bellini was nearly upon them. Aunt Luisa, sitting nearest the dance floor, was able to reach up and with much force pull her sister into a seat.

With one hand Aunt Luisa waved her glass at Ann and Minnie, still smiling.

"Yoo Hoo. You girls!"

Her other hand, under the table, had a firm grip on her sister.

"Luisa! Stop it. Let me up!!"

Luisa continued to beam. Her glass was lifted high, frothing and full. Ann turned back to Minnie and grinned.

"Somehow, I don't think we've got the full story on your aunt."

Luisa's glass spilled over just as Minnie reached up and kissed Ann quite expertly on the lips.

Blowing Glass

A S M A L L, slender young woman was latched firmly to Rosie's arm one night as she strolled beaming into Lassie's Bar. It looked like Rosie had found her oyster again, the sweet salty flesh that may or may not succumb to her demands, depending on age and temperament. It had been six months since Rosie's last passion ran out on her. Rosie's friends could breathe great sighs of relief. Whew, yeah! Rosie's got someone, have you heard? Rosie without a lover was an indignant host whose party has run out on her. She needed a skilled hand in her kitchen or else crockery managed to get smashed.

"Paula, could you get us a drink from over there. See the bar?"

Paula took off on a mission and Rosie stuffed her wallet back into her pocket. She always shouted. Always. Lee said that only once did she manage to buy Rosie a drink and that was when they were having a hootin' tootin' howler of an argument. I question the priority of buying a round at such a time but Lee assured me it had been necessary.

Rosie sat down, tugged up the collar on her expensive leather, beamed at us and said, "Well, what d'you think of my gorgeous new love? Maybe I shouldn't have let her go to the bar on her own. Tee hee."

Lee leaned across the table. "Do her parents know she's out?"

"What?"

"You could be had for child molestation."

"Or carnal knowledge."

"Hey, listen, Paula's nineteen years old. She's an art student — a very good one — and she lives with other art students in a terrace in Marrickville. Incredibly grotty. Why do students insist on ground-in dirt when they sign leases? They sit around and have intelligent conversations. I know because I've heard them. You should hear what kids talk about these days. Jesus! Her parents live in Orange and they know she's a dyke." Rosie scowled, "Not that I should have to justify my life to you two smug bastards."

"You know what we mean. All your other gorgeous new loves were your age. This one's fresh from puberty."

"She's had two relationships already."

"Who with, the gumnut babies?"

Rosie gathered herself to blast our scepticism to hell but Lee put her arm on Rosie's sleeve. "Put down your lance, Sir Galahad. Here come our drinks."

Paula had four gin and tonics on a tremulous lead.

Rosie liked a good kick up and a long drink, she had the sort of job in welfare that warranted hard play and good quality gin with it. She made me feel diluted somehow, as if I were a paler version of life with my careful I mights and moderate drinking.

"I didn't know if you wanted ice, so I said yes."

Rosie pulled Paula down next to her. "You did well, my love. Tell these two bad-tempered old women what you're doing at tech. Christine attempts to make music but it's been a while since she was close to anything vaguely creative. Lee doesn't count because she works in advertising."

I reached for the gin I didn't want and was overwhelmed by a sudden flashback to my first real relationship. The first crush on a woman that actually travelled the road of romance, heartbreak, desolation and wisdom after the act. She was twenty nine, my school teacher. I was seventeen and starting university. Sandra had sensed some sort of confused talent. Sandra flaunted me at parties, where I said nothing and smiled a lot. "Tell so-and-so what you're writing. Tell them what you're up to at uni." I had complied and performed like Shirley Temple tussling with a weighty monologue. Eventually her interest became vaguer and vaguer until pleasant jokes about our age difference became a reality. I left the relationship with an instilled desire to please which sat badly with the guilty clenchful of anger in my stomach.

Paula smiled at Rosie and took a drink from her glass. "We're looking at image," she said. "We're looking at people's self-perceptions and how they relate to big business and media. That sort of stuff."

She was all right, this one, I envy. She wasn't going to let anyone push her where she didn't want to go. At her age, she had an easy sociability that had taken me years to develop.

"What do you think you'll end up doing?" Lee asked.

"I really want to be a glassblower. I'd like to own a gallery and exhibit my work."

Rosie plonked her glass down on the table "That's not the best part, though," she shouted.

I've been told that we search for ourselves in our lovers. Rosie had been looking for a kid to complement her own open good nature. And now she brimmed with something delicious and she glanced sideways at the now more adult Paula with adoring complicity.

"Paula's going to slap the tired old women's movement and the art world on their arses. Women are going to start talking about sex again."

Paula held Rosie's hand. Her child.

"I mostly blow glass women in various positions. A lot of the time they're just lying together but sometimes they're kissing, or making love."

"Fucking," Rosie said. In case we hadn't understood.

"Ah yes. Fucking," Lee said thoughtfully. Paula and I laughed. It was like glass, tinkling. We were laughing like glass. Nice but fragile.

Paula and Rosie got up to dance. Someone had fed dollar after dollar into the jukebox, coaxing out what sounded like a chronological trip down memory lane. Fifties, now sixties.

Paula danced without thought, all instinct and fluidity. She didn't waste energy, but she managed to sway and shimmy and flirt with Rosie all at once. Rosie always flirted with the entire room when she danced. With this new lover she must have felt like she was dancing on air, with the clear, effortless joy that comes with a perfect night.

They moved towards each other and then danced backwards. Their approach was gentle, as if they sensed that the relationship wouldn't take much stress.

Now it was all three-minute top forty — happy music — and the floor was dense with bodies. Cigarettes were stubbed out on leather heels and drinks melted on the tables.

Lee and I sat in a comfortable silence, on the edge of this Saturday night and I wondered, as I always did, why we bothered to leave our cats, books and expensive house to sit in a carpet-lined smoke box.

"Where do older dykes go nowadays, darling?" I asked.

"They throw dinner parties and talk fondly about their lovers who are

10

studying architecture or doing NOW courses."

"God, you become more cynical every hour."

"Or if they want to dance they go to Pearls on the other side of the harbour."

"Why don't we go there?"

"We did go there but Rosie was wearing sneakers, 'member? They wouldn't let us through the door. Anyway, the drinks are expensive and you might meet some new woman there. Then you'd move out and I'd have to stay at home and listen to Rosie talk about how wonderful Paula is."

"Hmmm." Lee cuddled up. "You think they won't last? Maybe Rosie will get tired of all that blown glass."

"No! Paula will put her art first. Rosie'll hit the pots for a bit but she'll find someone else. Her own age."

I turned away from the dance floor, my eyes were sore and flooded with red light, and caught a sudden reflection in one of the mirrors. I peered closer at the glass and watched as my face became younger and rounder, my eyes anxious and dark. Was it a trick of the light? I looked twenty. I drew back, slowly, and I became thirty five again. Laugh lines came back and my skin looked like it was tired and wanted to go home. Lee, sprawled next to me, was a dark unchanging shape, innocent of this game I was playing. I closed my eyes, the light faded to black and I imagined a cluttered workshop, the sort of tableau that I've always wanted — where everything is within reach and a lush garden grows just outside. There was a skylight and red grainy wood formed the sloping ceiling. There was no telephone. Tables held paper and pencils in neat stacks and a draughting board sloped up against one brightly lit corner.

This was bliss, indeed. I was standing in the middle of the room, looking as I had when I was twenty, totally preoccupied, wrestling, if one could wrestle, with some new gust of glass-blowing energy. And there was Rosie, sitting in a chair in a corner near the greenly growing garden. She dangled a cigarette from one hand and wore a red flannelette shirt. and where was I in all this? I leaned forward in this half dream to catch hold of it all and miss nothing. Ah there! The whole studio watched as I tussled with art, helping it escape. Not a scrap of reticence. Great breasts ballooned out of the liquid silver and came to set with large nipples at their end. A big earth mother stomach took shape as well, bobbing gently in front of my mouth. It was a women's shape, transparent and large. The glass was the only vulnerable element.

Then the glassblower became Paula, smiling at her work, setting the little figurine down. I heard Rosie's voice and the studio faded and disappeared. "Hot out there! Paula, I'm going to buy you a drink. And something for Lee and Chrissie as well. Hey, listen you two, I want to drink to this kid. She's got taste. Chris, she wants to use you as a model. Lee, your girlfriend is going to be immortalised in glass."

Lee touched my face and my eyes opened onto the same night, shining with fresh promise. It was like light prismed through glass.

GINA SCHIEN: Writing fiction used to be a ragged, messy business for me and fitting it into my life was even messier. Playing drums in bands was a more creative hit and it came with team-work, friends, travelling and showing off in public.

Writing alone in a small room couldn't be more different and less glorious — solitude, hiding from noise and slow uncertain windings down dark unexplainable paths. I enjoyed getting stories published but I hovered between music and writing for years. I realised I would be treading water until I chose one over the other. This year I decided to concentrate on writing and suddenly it was no longer messy. It was pure. I welcomed the solitude. I liked what I learned about myself. (And I still play drums in the Gay and Lesbian Big Band once a week!)

Blowing Glass was written in 1989, while I was still hovering and while I was still agonising about my impending thirties — a strange time. It was influenced by Edmund White's writing. Minnie Gets Married was written in 1992 when the writing decision was on the horizon and being in my thirties just meant that I wasn't in my forties yet. It was inspired by the video of an Italian wedding — my girlfriend's son was the best man. I haven't actually been to a wedding since I was eight or nine.

Gina's lover on Gina: She has endured my children's growth from childhood through to adolescence, most of it with a smile. She's endured my working-class cynicism about what she calls the 'creative process' which I call wanky arty stuff.

She has endured living with someone who is part of that often hated profession (town planning) and who gets excited about footpath structures and textures.

Her ability to endure is what makes her unique.

The Euphoric Pleasure of Speech

WHEN I was seven, my aunt gave me a present. You. She had found you by the roadside. Wrapped in swaddling clothes. She swapped you on a whim, for a violin I'd always wanted. The old crone took the fiddle, and the two gold coins and smiled a toothless smile. She couldn't believe her luck. As my aunt wrapped you in her voluminous cloak and led you away, the crone never looked your way again.

At least, that's the way I'd always imagined it to be.

When I saw you standing there, on my doorstep, I cried. Not for you. Not out of pity. I cried for me and stamped my foot.

"What's wrong?" my aunt demanded. "I thought you'd like a brother."

I glowered and thundered. Tried to drive you from the room with my stare. And you just stood there, a dirty bastard child, a thief between worlds. You never blinked an eye.

Naturally, you became my obsession. You shouldn't be surprised. We were made from the same thing. Wove from the same welt. Both warped. Spun out and spinning round. Our hearts were matching peonies shot with purple.

I was your sister. We made that pact in blood and bruises. A language we both understood. One two three. "Swear," you said, and so I did. "Cunts," I said, "Goddamn fucking cunts." I laughed. Liberated. My aunt slapped me and called me a hog.

"Oink," I said. "Oink oink." We laughed so hard we pissed ourselves. Warm as melted butter, running down our legs.

We hung upside down from the weeping willows. The branches bent and almost touched the water with our weight. We blew, and watched our reflections shatter, merge and move on.

You wanted to touch the sweet earth, and press your fingers deep inside it where worms turned slow and blind. Instead, we swallowed the sky whole and burped it into stoppered glass jars.

You were my brother. My tongue was sharper than a knife and as keen. Mean. I tested it out on people. My words cut them up bad. I used the blunt end to draw pictures in the sand. But I was a secret romantic. I dreamt of fields lit only by the bright ruby flush of poppies, bigger than my fist. I was a secret romantic, dreaming of pale, wild eyed iconoclasts.

My hair was long, long. It caught and meshed the light. There was nothing in the world so black as my hair. One day, while I was asleep, you took a knife and cut it off. You wound it round your head. A prank, you said. I would have sliced you in half like salami, punched you in the mouth, but the sun felt good so close to the bone.

My aunt locked me up for that.

"You're turning into a tomboy," she said. "A desperado. What if the wind changed and you grew up to be a man?"

I was locked away without supper. I don't know for how long. The day's shadows lengthened and turned blue as broken hearts. I curled in a corner. I wished I was a spider. I wove a sticky web. Then I hung it from the moon bright trees and climbed down. You crouched in the middle like a vulgar sticky fly.

The night was full of Singapore rain.

When you were thirteen, you told me all your secrets. I chewed lemons and wasn't surprised. Not even by the story of the sailor. You met him in cold ditches by moonlight. You lusted for the smell of his boot, the taste of his cum delivered in the back of your throat. You were going to marry him, and run away to sea. He had a wooden leg, but you couldn't be sure you hadn't imagined the scarlet parrot on his shoulder.

The afternoon my aunt found you sprawled across his naked body you were salt white with desire. My aunt sent you away, after that.

I kissed your pale lips in farewell. Like a chaste sister. Like a nun. I wrapped the remnants of your last supper in a spotted scarf. You mustered all the sorrow of a tragic heroine, and disappeared into the sun.

My aunt looked at me then, and for the first time in years, smiled. She felt in the folds of her monstrous gown, disturbing years of dust. She produced a fiddle. Bright and shiny. I scraped it against my teeth, made vulgar splendid noises. The violin wailed like mourning women. I cast a veil over my face and vowed never to speak again.

Time passed. How? Fast. Slowly. I got a life. Took it. Shook it. I crossed rivers and swam in strange, warm seas. I was tired of being up to my ankles in storm water drains.

I fell in love.

On a wet seascape in September.

She was selling T-shirts. Film noir heroines and comic strip heroes.

Her eyes were wet and envy green. The colour of reef turtles.

She asked me my name. I wrote it in the sand with a stick. She sealed it with a kiss. X marks the spot. Then she disappeared over the dunes. A wet wolfhound, stiff with salt and panting, followed morosely in her wake.

Later that night I saw her in a pub. She was leaning over a black beer. She had fuck off hair, redder than the lips of John the Baptist. Her skin was soft and paper thin. A patrician daughter gone wrong. Hardly my type. And yet I bought her a drink and bent to kiss her mouth. She tasted of too-ripe berries. Later, she slid her latex fist into my cunt, drawing honey.

And I? I gave in at last to the euphoric pleasure of speech.

When at last she left me I turned stone still and sullen. My heart was empty and I had forgotten how to feel.

Years passed.

I sometimes thought of you. A flushed ghost. A distilled spirit. I diluted you and made you water.

Years passed. How? Slowly. Fast.

My aunt phoned me. Just like that. After seven years of silence. "Hello? Anyone there?" It wasn't love on the line. She said, "I bring you grievous tidings." She was Dickensian in more ways than one.

She told me you were dying.

I said — nothing.

There was nothing left to say.

"I feel it's my duty to tell you," she said, "AIDS. What else would it be?"

I put the phone down in her ear. Fuck her. Fucker.

But if I'd wanted to speak I couldn't have.

There were no words to describe what I might have said.

The room where you lay was filled with moving light.

My aunt bent over you. In the dark, her eyes glittered. She swayed like a mongoose, and smiled a vulture smile.

When you failed to die on cue, to do it the proper way, she took me by the hand and led me away.

"Sickness becomes him," she whispered to me. "He shines bright as a god."

I remembered you bright with desire, the sweet bootleather smell of your first pirate love, and hit her.

Hard.

Her eyes above her bloody handkerchief were blue and surprised.

It was the hottest night of the year, as I recall.

My aunt left messages on the answering machine. Saying nothing. There was no eloquence in her grim silences. Her promise to forgive us, to pray for us, left me cold. But I have the long memory of gangsters and sinners. Fuck me over and pay for it. My anger lodged sideways like a wishbone in my heart.

I drank gin and water and felt the sweat bead between my thighs.

I curled into a corner. I was delighted to discover that like a spider, I still knew how to spin. I drew the strands slowly from within, and started weaving, mucous gold.

I let myself slowly out of my hotel room. Pulled on my jacket and helmet. I let the engine out full throttle, and took off, across the badlands, yammering like a wolf, and hoping that if God was listening, he would disintegrate under the crushing weight of his own shame.

Paper tiger.

I blew on him and made him air.

You were pacing the floor when I got there. You were surprised to see me at the window. Your room was fifteen floors high.

I gestured silently to the window. Pulled at the thread that promised bright escape to the land below.

It was finer than a single hair.

"Oh no," you said, "not that."

"Trust me," I said. The thread was hempen rope, strong in my hand.

When we got to the bottom of that terrible descent, we were exhausted. Across the city, by the sea, it was lighter, but the city plain still slept on, blissful in its ignorance, ugly in its pitch-roofed sacrosanct silence.

"Come on," you said, "Let's give these motherfuckers something to think about."

We kissed each others' pale lips for luck.

The night was old. We took off across the barren streets. Pulled picket fences from lawns like rotten teeth. And lay them down to spell our name. Q_U_E_E_R. Just to give God something to think about.

"No epitaph," you said, and I thought, "Baby, we're only just beginning. Let's burn this fucking city to the ground, raze it to clean earth."

Someone in a floral nightgown gestured from a window and shouted. "Fire! Murder! Vampires!" Somewhere, a siren.

"We are your worst nightmare," you yelled, and winked.

I closed my eyes and saw red. The sun. Revenge. Bloodletting. The colour of my true love's hair. Fields of poppies in high summer flushed fever bright and bigger than both our hearts. Strike one up for passion and desire, my love.

Far across the city where the sea started, storms lit up the sky. Doors slammed. Someone screamed. Pirate ships appeared on the horizon.

I thought I saw my aunt. I thought she dropped to her knees and begged for mercy. Perhaps she was praying. We shrugged and let her pass.

Her language was not ours. Her speech drowned, gibberish to silence, swept away by the monstrous storms.

Kirsty Machon is 24. She has been carving a small niche for herself, reading in several events at the Harold Park Hotel, as an editor and contributor in Between Us 3 *(UTS Writers Group 1990) and most recently as a reader at the Queer Hatters Tea Party.*

She has also been dabbling in freelance journalism and so knows more than is probably sensible about the Witch of Kings Cross. When not skulking in her day job, Kirsty moonlights as an AIDS activist with the AIDS Coalition to Unleash Power (ACT UP, Sydney). She despises AIDS careerists, people who tell her AIDS is not an issue for women, and humourless moralists. She is obsessed with cats and soup.

Kirsty would like to make enough money from freelance journalism to write independently. Her current project is a collection of short fiction with three other women.

The writers who have inspired her in the last year are Dorothy Allison, Tom Spanbauer and David Wojnarowicz, who know that great writing comes from risking yourself.

The Euphoric Pleasure of Speech *has been published in* BURN. *It is dedicated to queer activities and AIDS activists everywhere, and in particular to a close friend who has taught her that change is created when love, anger and passion meet. It is for those who understand the implications of silence and have taken the risks to find their own voice.*

Emily Hagg

The Nun's Story

"**I** 'M O F F to the Cathedral," said Sister Veronica loudly to the man sitting beside her as the double decker bus we were travelling on trundled past Taylor Square.

The entire lower deck could hear her. I turned away in embarrassment. She was always doing this to me. From our first day together in kindergarten at St. Ursula's Convent to the last day of sixth form, when she could hardly stagger off the stage at Speech Day with all the prizes she'd won, (Dux of the School, Captain of Hockey, St. Agnes Award for Civic Enterprise, The Elsie Meanine Medal for Choral Singing, etc) Sister Veronica's energy and enthusiasm remained constant, notable and infectious.

"A natural leader," Mother Andrew used to say proudly, looking out her study window onto the playing fields below where Sister Veronica in gymslip and sandshoes, rushed tirelessly up and down the sidelines urging her teammates on to greater efforts in tunnel ball practice. Four years had passed since our last day of school but Sister Veronica's unselfconscious passion for organising others remained as keen as ever.

So now the spectacles and sunburnt balding head of the man she had spoken to gleamed towards her in a friendly fashion.

"That's nice, Sister," he said. "I'm off to bowls myself. As you can see." He gestured self-consciously towards his cream and white wrappings.

"How long is it since you've been to Church?" demanded Sister Veronica sternly. The sunlight glinted across her large horn rimmed spectacles with a mesmerising effect.

"Well ... you know how it is ..." the bowler muttered uncomfortably. He looked up at her and then stared, transfixed, like a fly speared on a pin.

"My wife goes, and the kiddies," he offered placatingly. "My oldest girl's just started at St. Ursula's."

But Sister Veronica was unappeased.

"Typical, that's just typical. Leave religion to the women and children, eh?" Her voice was loud and sharp.

"No ... no ..." murmured the bowler in embarrassment. By now the entire lower deck was tuned in to the conversation. I thought I heard murmurs of agreement behind.

"How can the Church progress if its members take no interest?" demanded Sister Veronica, still in the same loud tone. "It's a disgrace."

"Quite right, Sister," said a fat woman sitting across the aisle from me and clacked her knitting needles decisively in affirmation. But everyone else was silent as Sister Veronica looked around for further signs of support.

"I wonder how many of you know what's happening at the Cathedral this morning?" she asked of the bus at large. There were indeterminate murmurs. Those unfortunately without books or papers stared hard out the window or at the floor. In the sudden awkward silence the words "bloody old crow" rang out clearly from the back. Sister Veronica was on her feet instantly, surging down the aisle in outraged billows of black and white to confront her critic, a pimply teenager in jeans and T-shirt who sneered limply in his seat as she towered over him.

"What did you say?" she demanded.

He muttered inaudibly.

"Go on — say it out loud so that everyone can hear you!"

The boy looked up to find every eye fastened on him and shrivelled with embarrassment. Pleased with the success of her standover tactics, Sister Veronica left him alone, swung back to face the rest of the lower deck and began to orate.

"Since none of you seem to know, I'll tell you all exactly what's happening at the Cathedral this morning. There's a Gay Rights demonstration on behalf of a young teacher who was sacked from St. Mark's last week because he's a homosexual. And now that you all know, I hope that some of you will join us. Because, according to my calculations, at least three of you on this bus must be gay as well. Time to come out of your closets!"

She gave the audience a big smile and a clenched fist salute, ignoring the protests that were starting to break out around her. The woman with the knitting needles was reaching for the conductor's bell.

I looked at my neighbour's face. Her jaw had dropped. (I'd always thought that that was a figment of the literary imagination.) But my observations were interrupted by Sister Veronica yelling at me, as the fat woman hammered on the bell and the bus began to grind to a halt.

"Sister Xavier, you slut, get your hand off that woman's breast and come with me!"

I followed hastily as she swung round the bar and jumped to the ground, then stood holding her up while she fell about laughing.

"Did you see their faces? ... oh jeez ... that woman next to you — when you started to sniff the lighter fluid ..."

"Come on," I said, "you're attracting attention. We have to keep going.

We're going to be late."

Sister Veronica shut up in mid-cackle. We walked sedately to the corner and waited for the lights to change. Two blocks away at the foot of the Cathedral steps an active patchwork of colour and movement and faint echoes of shouting indicated that the demonstration was underway. I felt the first cold wash of apprehension crawling swiftly over my skin.

But distraction was at hand.

"Routine B," snapped Sister Veronica as the lights changed and we started to cross the road.

"What?" I was asking as she grabbed me by the shoulders forcing me backwards in a passionate embrace over the bonnet of the taxi beside us. Brakes squealed behind.

"My God, look at that!" I heard as I did my best to mime frantic struggle and gradual ecstatic surrender in the short space of time available.

I was really getting into it when Sister Veronica suddenly let me go.

"Quick," she said, "the lights are changing." She skipped across the road and I followed, straightening my veil. The taxi honked furiously and Sister Veronica made a rude gesture from the safety of the kerb.

"Come on," she said. "I can hear them shouting." So could I. We hurried down the street as fast as our habits would allow. As we came nearer I saw that the bulk of the crowd of demonstrators was gathered round the wrought-iron gates and the stone wall at the bottom of the flight of steps leading up to the Cathedral. More than half of them were trapped between the wall and the encircling line of uniformed police at the top of the steps who, moving slowly forward with their arms linked, were gradually forcing the crowd back out through the gates. Still a block away, I saw a scuffle break out at the top of the steps and heard a renewed clamour of outraged shouting. Sister Veronica started to run.

"Look, it's the Flying Nun!" said a small boy wheeling his bike down the street.

"Stuff you, mate," snarled Sister Veronica in passing. She was well ahead of me now. She was a faster runner and managed the cumbersome skirts with more finesse. By the time I arrived at the back of the crowd I had lost sight of her. Craning over people's heads trying to see, I became entangled with two old ladies with shopping trolleys who, seemingly unaware of the situation, were trying to get up the steps to the Cathedral.

"Make way there," said one of them crossly, poking the man in front of her in the small of his back with her umbrella.

"Can't you see that the Sister's trying to get through?" As he turned round and glared at me resentfully I realised to whom she was referring.

"Thank you, my dear," I murmured, as I started to push past. "Excuse me. Excuse me." The demonstrators muttered but gave way. The crowd opened and closed in again behind me like a snake ingesting its prey. My heart began to pound as I pushed and was pushed by the pressure of bodies behind, towards the front. Arriving in the second line of demonstrators I looked up and saw Sister Veronica only a few feet away in front of me suddenly break loose from the crowd. With the swift swooping trajectory of an attacking galactic invader or a vital return throw from the boundary she went leaping up the steps in a wild diagonal across the police line, yelling at the top of her voice, "Sisters! Come out of your closets!"

Two policemen dived backwards, grabbed her wrists and ankles and hurled her bodily down the stairs. I looked down, horrified, but she'd fallen on other demonstrators and they were all picking themselves up and laughing. Two more police began to advance from the lines at the back of the crowd towards her. As they did so, I saw one of the old ladies who had helped me through the crowd rush at them with her umbrella, crying, "How dare you treat a nun like that!"

The chanting in front had suddenly died. I was still in the second line, now forced back almost to the wall, but I was part of a small group caught on the wrong side of the gate, trapped between its tall iron spikes and the unyielding wall behind. Glancing round for the last time I saw Sister Veronica being manhandled off towards a waiting paddy wagon by one policeman, while the other tried to placate the old ladies. It didn't look as though she'd make our afternoon rendezvous at a rerun of *The Sound of Music*. All the jaffas we'd bought to roll down the aisle would be wasted. And there'd be extra rental to pay on the habits if we didn't get back to Custom Costumes on time. But now I had more immediate problems. Looking forward again I saw that one of the policemen who'd thrown Sister Veronica down the steps was glaring straight at me and starting to move forward. I thought that the time had come to leap over the wall.

EMILY HAGG: Lives in Sydney. Works as a lawyer. Dreams of the sea. Enjoys: children, family, friends, seafood, dry white wine, Anthony Trollope, white water rafting, sixteenth century music. Has failed to master: the dialectic, relationships or clutter management. Wants to write a good play, lose weight and see Salzburg.

It Could Have Been

I T C O U L D have been the office party although that sounds like a cliche. But don't you love cliches. She was drunk and smiled wider and wider and got softer and softer. My boss. Really. She talked and talked and touched. And then I had to leave. I was going somewhere else, out into the cold night, the city, traffic, Friday night drinking with friends and already half full.

So I didn't think about it at the time. You see, I have a lover and we're happy. And my boss is a red-blooded heterosexual, married, two kids and not someone to put a foot wrong. Too often.

And we always got on OK. I knew her from somewhere else. Before she was my boss. So we could refer to things outside — it wasn't just a relationship centred on this one workplace.

She would touch but lots of people do that. It's nice and I don't mind it. From women, that is. And we worked well together. She'd get ideas. I'd twist them around into other ideas. That's work, that's what I do. The city rolled and washed outside, the glint of light from the river, the traffic, the mass movement of the work brigades, the new coloured glass buildings.

Then there was another party, a farewell. One of the typists leaving. And someone bought some champagne and we all kept drinking it and the division head dropped in and tried to put his arm around her shoulder and she dipped down and around away from him and grabbed my arm and a bottle of champagne and pulled me around a corner to the lifts, laughing. And she moved so quickly, her lips so lightly touched mine as, still laughing, she reached past me to the lift button. And pressed.

And then we were on the top floor, the open conference area, talking about this and that. And somehow she had two glasses. She poured and we drank and walked to the windows, looking out into the city which was sliding from grey into bright night. She still had my arm and I didn't know what to do. I had a feeling I shouldn't be there. I didn't quite understand. But I was on 'go' all of a sudden. And that's where I should have stopped.

She stopped. By the window. Looking out, she spoke. "You like the night, don't you?" And then looked at me, and smiled, much too slowly. While my mind raced at light speed, or faster. "Night's fine," I said and put my hands deep into my pockets. But they didn't stay there long. You know how it is.

I must say, in all fairness, that she was good. And was it her first time? I don't know. Of course, we were a bit drunk but not drunk enough to blame champagne. She is smaller than me but that night I discovered she had flesh, in all sorts of places. And lips everywhere too, it seemed. So I guess that means we took off our clothes. Slowly. I'm sure it was slow. And her breasts, those solid nipples. And her hand inside me. And all those lips, and the wet, and the moving, again and again and again.

Just once, sharply, the sound of voices and laughing. We stopped breathing, one very long moment, hovering and silent and still. And the voices faded and we plunged back into each other bodies.

Then we lay still for a while, side by side, and got cold so we dressed. Again slowly. There was the taste and smell and feel of saliva, cunt, sweat and alcohol all over us. She laughed and said, "I think I'd better wash this off before I go home." At that moment I seemed to wake up and the night began to die. And I realised that I would have to tidy myself up as well.

Stray lust is a strange game and I didn't know what to expect the next Monday. When I would have to see her. It turned out like any other Monday. She was friendly but matter of fact and said nothing about what happened. There was no gossip either. But I watched her secretly. She was a little softer, I thought, or even a little broken or sad. I don't know, even now. It didn't make sense.

I guess I should have felt used. I tried to sometimes. Then sometimes it all seemed irrelevant. Because, didn't I tell you, I was happy.

One month later she announced to us that she was leaving. Job in another city. And one more time, much more soberly and much more discreetly, she asked me to come, she took me, at night, to a place where we made love, we fucked, we used each other up. It was serious, harder, tougher. She might have even cried but I'm not sure.

And we talked a bit although I don't remember what we were saying. I think she was just trying to say goodbye. And I think I was trying to trace a message in her body.

23

Walking Into Your Room

T H E P O S T C A R D of Judy Garland is intense — the eyes and the lips — stuck on your pinboard above your desk. All the pictures of women leap out from their cardboard masks and stare at me staring at them from the doorway.

It's the feeling you get walking into a bar — the eyes and the lips and the intensity of lust and alcohol, desperation and bonding. That was where I met you, circulating through a cloud of feminists and smoke. You were laughing like you meant it, which was why I thought I might like you. But I didn't touch your skin until six months later, here, as you led me in the door pretending to be drunk. You soon got over that. You were sane and passionate but still soft somewhere.

So, today, I lean a moment against the wooden door jamb, also a portal to the new world I have been travelling in. The crowds, the parties, the bars just now seem irrelevant, but necessary and inscribed clearly on my newsreel imagination set running by the first piercing gaze of Judy's singing eyes.

I push out into your room and the crowded noticeboard faces settle into their usual flatter planes. I try not to trip on your shoes. Your accompaniments slip on and off you easily — it makes me tremble sometimes. The first time you were unfaithful I disappeared for weeks. The second time you said "hold me only, don't hold on to me". I still think that's shit, and I told you so then, but I hold you and make of it what I can.

On the bedside table there is a leather-bound notebook — your diary, some of your thoughts. I am tempted. You sleep on. The leather cover is scuffed in some places, rubbed smooth in others. I run my hand over the surface. I do want to read it because you still constantly surprise me. But I know I won't, because you could still surprise me and I'm not sure today I could bear being surprised.

Now I reach down and pick up a child's book by your cast-off sand-shoe. They still make Little Golden Books. You say your ex-lover's child is a little golden thing — one of your ex-lover's, the one before me. You have your own sort of loyalty. "We made a deal when we were together about this kid," you said. At first, I remember, I resented baby-sitting, being spattered with creamed spinach, having my hair pulled, wanting to scream after having sung 'Old MacDonald' twenty times with every animal sound, not one missed. I was growling like a tiger. But the little golden girl loves me, despite all that. One day I realised this and I burst into tears. After that I was gone.

We are strange nonbiological mothers, unreliable, indifferent at times, but at other times needing the fleeting intrusion of love and play from your ex-lover's kid. This is a book I bought for her. I don't get tired, mostly, of reading it now.

But today I put it down. I have come to see you. I step over your clothes — jeans, T-shirt, socks, knickers. You are on the bed turned away, asleep. You are bound up in the sheets but now free of clothes. I will now free you of the sheets as well. I will take you instead to the place where you will take me, to where there is some freedom, and some binding up of spirits by hands and lips and sounds. The sounds of us will soon be loosened in this space and it doesn't matter who is watching.

ANGELA MYSTERIOSO: Writing is my way of talking to the world. The people in my stories are always talking, and walking, through a world cluttered with icons, memory and possibility. I'm also fascinated and chilled by organisations. Walking into Your Room, of course, isn't true, but I've heard stories a bit like it. Judy Garland, however, does exist.

About me: I love music, especially jazz (Coltrane, Miles, Sandy Evans) and drink too much coffee. I'm a magician: I can make a bottle of single malt scotch last a year. Life's tough these days, it's the '90s. But I don't believe a woman should go down any mean streets. There are better ways of going down. I guess I'm waiting till the real thing comes along. Meanwhile, back to the keyboard, back to the screen through which I speak. And the mysterious angels.

The Lobster Queen

I DON'T know what I thought of her then. I know that the details don't matter. It could have been any two women, a thirty-year-old, a fourteen-year-old, falling in love, on a wharf anywhere in the world. Chinese women, for instance. They were very cold. They held each other through their coats, on the wharf.

The older one always woke early and had her first cup of tea by five-thirty. She had ironed a hanky and put it in the pocket of the coat she loaned the girl. On the wharf later the girl put her hand in the pocket. It was still warm.

It may have been a year after when the girl's father found a letter she had hidden in a sock. She had forgotten writing it. Later she realises there are forgotten areas all through her history, spread like fishing nets over the landscape, nets which turn to clouds so areas of nothingness occur. The empty territory of the psyche. In this country the body blurs sideways from the shock of what the nothing must contain.

We are not the same women we were. Everything has changed. When I looked back I could remember some things about the girl. I know there are major blur areas. At this point the details do matter.

In summer they began to fish from a rusted wreck at the end of the breakwater. It was dangerous to walk on, especially in the half-light before sunrise. They were usually the only ones there. At low tide they walked to the bottom of the ship and fished for yellowtail swimming in the hold. The girl said she was tempted to dive in, the water was so green. Her friend said, "Don't be crazy, there's sharks."

The woman stood up and rigged her rod with a live yellowtail and cast into the sea. When she caught her first tailor, she filleted it and used that to bait both lines. "Tailor eat tailor," she said to the girl, casting again in one smooth action.

Every movement the woman made, the girl copied her. At first she cast so wildly the hook swung behind her and caught her trousers. They were laughing into each other's faces, in a light nor'-easter wind.

"Here," the woman said, and she took the hook out. Then slowly she turned the girl around and kissed her on the mouth.

"Do it properly," the girl said. "You know what I mean. Kiss me properly."

The deck of the *Adolf*, wrecked in 1907 on top of six other ships, swayed beneath her. She held the woman for balance, and breathed in her breath. She tasted of sea wind and being outside and early light.

The woman looked at her for a long time, at first with a hot longing, then sadly, and then, with a kind of line across her face she bent to pick up her rod and demonstrated the cast. The girl watched each movement, the tanned fingers releasing the reel clip, the slow backward arch of the back, the forward movement as she cast out so far the sinker was a tiny plop, invisible. The arms straight, strong, exactly in the direction where she wanted the bait to land. She did all this without speaking, then squatted and lit a cigarette.

Waiting for the schools of tailor to come in was like all waiting, a suspension, a positive quietness of the body, the tingling edge of any part of her body knowing it would leap at a movement of the line.

"How will I know," the girl asked, "whether it's waves moving the line, or a fish?"

"Your fingers will become sensitive," the woman said, showing her how to rest the line on the tip of her index finger, teaching her when to wind in a bit, when to let it out.

When the first tailor hit the line they stood and braced themselves, the sensation of a fish was so definite after all, and for twenty minutes they were reeling them in, shining and white, taking them by the gills and unhooking them, casting again. Sometimes they forgot to rebait the hook, everything went so fast, and they caught fish anyway, by the fin, by the gills, because the school was so thick.

After the catch, fifteen or twenty fish at that time of year, they squatted to clean them. The girl watched the woman's fingers fly, scales lifting to the air like sequins, the knife expertly opening the belly, guts being flicked into the sea, the carving of fillets, never a mistake, the roe sacs of pregnant ones, blood on the fingers, sometimes the birds collecting, surrounding them.

The woman let down a bucket on a rope and hauled up water from the hold. They washed the fish. Squatting either side of the bucket they stared at each other, the girl's green eyes soaking blue from the woman's, till the woman leaned back and put her hands to her face. She breathed in, looking through her fingers at the girl, and smiled, shaking her head slightly, wry. At this time the girl knew what the gesture meant, without knowing why.

There would be more waiting at the house. Waiting was a part of everything that happened. The girl waited on the step, or on the chiller near the door, while the woman made tea in an aluminium pot.

Sometimes she disappeared to do other things and the girl didn't know where she was. Sounds would tell her — the dog barking at a man who came in asking for a haircut, water running, a bath being run.

"Get in," the woman said to the girl, "I'll come later and wash your back."

In the car, on the lounge watching TV, she held her hand out to the girl. At sundown she opened a bottle of beer and began to cook for the men. She walked the girl home at night. Before they came to the gate she took the girl's head in her hands, holding her face she kissed her once, not 'properly', but breathing in, holding the breath.

In winter the girl stayed in the kids' room once or twice, when the kids were away. In the bed they opened mouths, necks, arms, bellies, but there were places the girl could not touch her, these were her frozen zones, this was what she told the girl. Something is wrong, but nothing is ever explained. Later the girl will write the letter and hide it, unable to post it in case the opening of questions closes everything that has happened. She will hide it in a sock, and forget it. It will not exist.

At certain times of the year they went up the river in a long rowboat the woman hired from Mr Lindstrom, the dwarf. He lived in a small house he'd built himself opposite the mangrove flats, and kept bait in two long freezers. A wooden ladder leaned against each freezer, and sometimes the dwarf sat on one of these ladders while his customers worked out where they would fish, and what bait would be needed. He would recommend one thing or another depending on the wind and the tide. There was a windsock in his front yard and a hand-painted notice saying PIPPIES. CHICKEN GUTT. WORMS. PRAWNS. YELLOWTAIL.

It was early winter and there was frost on his lawn. The girl stopped at the small door and looked back at the marks their sandshoes had left in the frost. They bought the packets of bait and he followed them across the road to the river. The woman thanked him and headed out along the jetty. He stood there watching her movements, the darting of a cormorant behind her, smoke from the industries across the river, then ripples in the mudflats beneath them.

"This is not a rewarding liaison," the dwarf said flatly. The wispy curls on his large head shook themselves in the river breeze. He was standing on the bank, and the girl had stepped down onto the jetty, so they were looking directly at each other. The girl noticed his eyes had kind lines around them.

"I've asked her to go away with me," the girl said.

The dwarf looked out at the rowing boat, where the woman was storing the tackle bag, the buckets, the picnic.

"She won't go away. She had no family when she came here."

"I don't think she's happy."

"Who is happy? Tell me this. She will never take the children away."

The girl turned to look. The early light had turned the river pink. In the boat the woman sat quietly waiting

"You must find someone else to love," the dwarf said.

"It's too late."

"You will never get to know her."

"Maybe not. It doesn't stop the love."

"No."

"Does everyone know about us?"

"They have guessed. In the town they call you 'the boys'. They won't say anything."

"There's nothing to say."

"No." The dwarf took her thin hand in his pudgy one and held it softly. His white hairs lifted and settled again on his head. "Tell her to take you up into Fullerton Cove," he said, "to the whiting hole. She knows where it is."

They have lit a fire on the beach, and cooked a schnapper for lunch. The woman turns to sit facing the sea and lights a cigarette. She smokes it without saying anything. The girl considers how these two years have happened. She is sixteen and nothing has changed, there are no explanations.

Her fingers are not as sensitive as the woman's. She has learnt to tell the difference between the way a tailor and a bream take the hook; how a flathead is exciting, sudden, and swims hard, how a crab will suck and so on. She has learnt the woman's language, which she will forget later, but now seeing a man further down the beach dragging a fish on a rope and bending, rising, putting worms in the tin on his waist she says, "Must be whiting about." The woman nods.

The woman has not much use for words. Most of her talk is saved for the dog, and the girl has learnt that a mood can be judged by this. If the woman is happy with the girl she will speak to the dog with such affection and endearments the girl is sure it's for her.

"You darling thing. Look at those beautiful eyes. Come here now and let me cuddle you, gorgeous thing you are. What a girl!"

At other times the dog sits under the table, waiting, till the woman says "I don't want to SPEAK to you." None of her moods seem to be related to anything, as far as the girl can see.

On the beach the woman put her cigarette out and said, "My mother was a good swimmer." There was a long silence.

"She was in the state team, before she had me. They said," (she looked down towards the wreck, towards the city) "they didn't know who my father was. I think he was rich, but he never came near her again after I was born, except once when I was in the Home."

The girl considered this information carefully. It was the longest speech the woman had made in the time she had known her.

"Why were you in the Home?" the girl asked.

"My mother died when I was one," the woman said.

Suddenly she had lost her straight back, she seemed smaller than before. The girl wanted to take her in her arms.

Could she be reached out for? She was staring straight out to sea. The girl moved and sat in front of her. Now they had locked vision. The woman's eyes had turned into wells reflecting the sea, the fine lines radiating to the edge of the iris seemed painted there like markings on a lizard. She kept her eyes focused on the girl and made slight movements of her head from side to side. Eventually she looked away and lit two cigarettes. She passed one to the girl.

The girl smoked the cigarette because it tasted like the kiss. How many thousands of cigarettes she smoked later because of the memory of the kiss.

The girl realised she was on some sort of path. The way was not clear, but there was a fellow traveller. Later the path would be crowded with women but the girl was not to know this. When she looked ahead now she saw two solitary figures, parting and coming together again, but always parting.

She thought about the woman's mother. The woman could not let herself be held, by a friend, by a *child,* whom she now turned to abruptly — "I want you to swim," she said. "Go and get in the water."

The girl put down the schnapper bone she was sucking on and walked towards the water. There was a boat in the distance, too far away to see her clearly. She took off her jeans and jumper and stood naked for a while, breathing, telling her body not to feel the cold. She bent to a low dive and stroked out to the first wave, which went over her like a tunnel. Underwater she opened her eyes and saw how green it was, a yellow green light like columns of buildings in other civilisations, then the discrete grains of sand, each one with its edges and vertices. She breast-stroked along the bottom, holding her breath as long as she could — almost a minute— and then came up to face the horizon, gasping slowly so it wouldn't show, and continued out beyond the waves. There was *The Lobster Queen,* the boat her friend was never allowed to go on because it belonged to her husband, and women were thought to be bad luck on fishing boats.

The girl could see the husband and his deckhand moving about, shaking fish from the net. The men didn't look up.

30

She turned and arrowed back to the waves. Ahead of the breakers, she trod water and began to take deep breaths. When the wave was three lengths behind her she began to swim fast. The wave collected her like a giant hand and she ducked her head and held her arms straight out in front, fingers stretched. Then slowly she brought her arms back to her sides and came in fast on the beach, head first. The wave eddied and she stood up, an aviator, elated, the saltbush in the distance dancing, each leaf an oiled sparkling green.

"Don't you ever do that again," the woman said. "You had me frightened half to death, staying under so long."

The girl bent and nuzzled her face into the dog's neck, nuzzling and pretending to bite, then she dug her fingers in near the dog's tail and brought them backwards through the fur to the neck, growling, and the dog growled with her.

Late in the afternoon they went back to the beach for another throw. Squinting, the girl could make out cars on the breakwater and people fishing off the wreck. Then the woman had something on her line and reeled in fast.

"Huh, I thought it was a bloody fish, the way you pulled it in," the girl said. She stood looking down at a heap of tangled line on the hook.

"No, no. We can use this," the woman said. She had a hook in her mouth and the sun was shining on her eyebrows and teeth, on her straight nose. Her disappointed face.

The girl helped her undo the line, feeding the end through tangles, then holding it as the woman got progressively further away while unknotting it. Talking to herself about breaking-strain and bream. Then she came back and showed the girl how to tie it on to another line so it would be long enough.

"This is a blood knot, will you remember how to do it?"

"Yes."

"Will you remember how to do it when I'm dead?"

"Yes."

At seven o'clock the sheet of wet sand was streaked in pink and orange from the setting sun. The woman stood, a hand in her cardigan pocket, nudging at the sand with a toe. "Remember when we used to dig out pippies with our feet? Bucketfuls." The girl caught up with her and said, "Come on, let's walk." They went through wave edges and past an old man worming. He had a smelly piece of mullet tied on a string, and was dragging it across the sand after each wave receded. Every so often he bent down and pulled a long worm out of the sand, and dropped it in a tin tied to his belt. His rod was standing upright in the sand further along. "Must be whiting about," the girl said. The woman grunted.

That night they went to the hotel and sat in the lounge bar with the other women. They played the jukebox and drank beer till late.

When the girl went to the toilet the woman followed her in and stood with her back to the door watching the girl pee. When the girl finished, the woman pushed her gently to the side wall and put her arms on the wall and brought her face close and kissed her on the mouth. Through the wall the girl could hear 'Put your sweet lips a little closer to the phone, Let's pretend that we're together, all alone' and in her mouth she could hear the woman humming the same song against her tongue and her teeth. Then the woman sat and peed, while the girl watched.

"You go out first," the woman said.

It was the first time the girl had been drunk, and she realised how many times she had seen the woman drunk and not recognised it. She also thought, as they were driving home, she could top the woman's drink up at night — that helping her get drunk would make things happen. Half the night she lay awake thinking about this, it was a moral decision she could make. Her body told her to do it. Her mind said no; her mind won.

In the morning when the girl came into the yard amongst the half-made lobster pots, fish traps, string nets, bits of planking, oil drums, she saw the woman on the step cleaning out her tackle bag. With a minimum of words, and slowing the action of her hands so the girl could follow, she showed her rigs for different fish, when to use a trace, a swivel, and what size sinkers were needed. Then she took the reels off and squatted and showed the girl how they worked, and how to clean and oil them.

"This is an egg-beater," she said, "and this is what the ratchet's for. This is an Alvey reel, or a sidecast. It's better for the beach."

The girl looked at this one — it was the classic type you saw in books with people fishing, a plain reel, made of bakelite like the old radios.

"I'll get one of these one day," the girl said.

The woman looked at her and said, "You'd be better with an egg-beater."

The girl ignored this. She would get what she wanted. It would never be just a matter of fishing.

Later the woman took her to the shed and showed her the sinker moulds, and pieces of lead they'd collected at the tip, or from people's roofs. They weighed the lead in their hands like butter. For some time they stood in the green light at the bench where her husband's cousin made their sinkers. 'My cousin' she called him, but the girl knew he was her husband's cousin. It was the tall man who came to have his hair cut in the kitchen.

The woman was in a good mood that morning. She talked quietly about the tides and times of year and what fish liked to eat. She talked about the different shapes of the insides of fish, she said that mullet could only be netted or jagged because they wouldn't take a hook, and how they had a black lining to their gut.

"Groper do this," she said, squatting on the lawn near her tomato beds, opening and closing her mouth as she brought her head closer to the girl, who leaned in, her hair brushed by a sheet on the washing line. The woman sat back, grinning, and said "Now that's enough."

"How is your boyfriend," she said, after a long time. "Do you have a boyfriend at work? What about the man who came into the restaurant?"

"I want you," the girl said. "Now."

"Now, now," the woman said, and went to fill the copper at the end of the shed. In the middle of the day her husband would come home. The shed had low windows at the back which let in the greenish light. Standing there watching, the girl realised that although the woman said she didn't have any love left for her husband, although they rarely spoke and then only to abuse each other, the abuse was the form their passion now took, it was their way of staying together, and the truth was the woman liked to do things for him — but only when he wasn't home. These things were done at certain times of the day — washing his overalls, filling the copper, ironing the shirts he wore to the club in the afternoons. The ironing lay on the floor in neat piles near her tools — the saw, hammer, chisels, brushes — things she needed to fix the house.

He kept his tools separate in the shed, where he spent most of his time when he wasn't on the boat. He had a kettle and tea things in the shed, where his friends visited him. He had a fridge there, and bales of wire and a cocky in a cage. When he came home he would stand in his overalls, wreathed in steam over the copper boiling his lobsters. Then he would take the catch to the co-op, come home and have a bath, put on his ironed shirt and go to the club and get drunk. He did this every day. At night he came home at ten, took his tea out of the oven and ate it alone, grumbling, while she watched the late news. They didn't do anything together except sleep in the same bed. Once the girl had sneaked into their bedroom. There were little piles of clothes everywhere, and the racing pages from the paper. The girl thought that maybe they had a flutter together now and then, but she would never know this. It was the permanent mystery of adults who seemed to choose not to be happy. They could not give up the things they had because the things were known and clear and warm. If they were warm with abuse it was just another kind of heat.

The girl could see that the man was jealous of her, and that he didn't know what to do about it. Sometimes as she passed the shed he growled at her, which was his way of saying hello, and she would smile and ask how he was, but usually he pretended she wasn't there. He listened to the races on his little radio.

Sometimes the kids tried to talk to him, but he would tell them to get out of his way, he said he was worried they'd get a hook in their foot, or put their hands in his copper of lobsters.

The girl thought he might be uncomfortable because the boy looked like a girl, and the girl looked like a boy, but she never knew. Her own father was not good at speaking to children. So the man seemed normal, but more so. She tried not to think about him. Once he asked if she would like a naughty and she said no and thanked him, and went away with her throat burning.

She had forgotten writing the letter to the woman, and not sending it. Who are we, what are we doing? she had asked. Why is this so strong? Where are the others? She had obviously hidden it in the sock. Her father was waving it in the air and speaking crudely, in his insulted state, and then he hit her once, hard, on the face. When she became conscious she was lying on the bed. He was continuing with his sentences.

Later her father went to visit her friend, trying three hotels and then the house. He told the woman he'd ring up the market where she worked and explain to them just what kind of person she was. He advised her never to touch his daughter again.

Ten years later the girl found out this had happened. She had rung her sister and the sister said, "Just like when Dad —" and the story came out.

"When did this happen?" she said, "this visit of Dad's — when I was sixteen? What — seventeen? When I was at the restaurant?"

"Look," her sister said. "I thought you knew. Didn't anyone tell you?"

"No, nothing," she said.

"Well, look. I think you were sixteen. I used to lie for you, say you'd gone to another friend's place. You were seeing her for two years, three years — were you doing it? You never said."

"I don't know. Not exactly. Not completely."

The phone call left her in shock for days. In the kitchen looking at her quince tree through a small pane of blue glass she understood why she'd hated her father. Or why the hate was as strong as the love. Before, her rage had been blind. Her father's face appeared and she bared her teeth.

So many years later, it became clear why the woman had suddenly turned cold towards her. When she visited, the woman would hardly acknowledge she was there. There was no news about which cousin had sunk someone's boat because that bloke had stolen lobsters from his traps. No affectionate talk to the dog who now sat on the girl's lap, or beside her on the step, as if to console her. There were the visits and there was silence. The woman never sent her away, and never said why she had changed. When the girl asked if something was wrong, the woman shrugged, and got up to make more tea.

Sometimes there were strange fish in the sink.

"What's this you've caught?" the girl said. She leaned over, smelling it.

"Trevally," the woman said.

"What did you catch it with?"

"Beach worms," the woman said, talking for a while about the habits of trevally.

When the girl tried to talk about things other than fishing, personal things, the woman was silent or changed the subject. She moved her lips around without opening her mouth. She shrugged a lot, and looked out the back door. She always had her hand on the brown dog beside her.

They sat looking at the husband's nets drying on stumps on the back lawn. The husband was watching his lobsters cook, and turning his head to the side now and then to say something to his cocky. He had found the cocky caught in wire on the riverbank, injured, and brought it home and nursed it for months. Sometimes he put the cocky on his shoulder, and fed it with cheese.

The woman made the girl tomatoes on toast and tea with milk and sugar. Then she opened the fridge and took out a lobster she'd taken from her husband's catch the day before.

"Come here," she said, beckoning with the lobster's feelers. At the bench she showed the girl how to open the lobster, laying it on its back and making a neat cut down the centre of the tail up to the head, and opening the shell away. Now she took a round segment from near the tail and held it to the girl's mouth.

The flesh was moist silk against her tongue. It was as though every sweet flathead fillet she'd ever eaten was a preparation for this craving in the mouth. They set to and devoured the lot, grasping legs and cracking them open and sucking out the flesh. They ate the lobster's brain. They up-ended the shell and drank the juice. Then they wrapped what was left and put it in the bin out of sight.

When they sat down again, the woman's face seemed to set in its lines till she looked like a statue. Sometimes this had happened at night, when she was tired. She sat very still, without speaking.

The dog came in and put its paws on the girl's lap, and looked into her face. Its eyes were a deep gold flecked with brown like a river stone seen through water. Eventually the woman said, "Maybe you ought to get a boyfriend. Don't you think?"

"If you want me to," the girl said.

The Frilling Machine

A T M Y school, as at all schools in those days, there was a frilling machine at one end of the playground. Australians telling their autobiographies are always describing the stand of pepper trees, their scent, the little red peppercorns, and what went on under the trees. As an innocent for a short amount of time, I also laid out twigs and round stones for the boundaries of my house, and made doorways for certain people to come in.

The frilling machine was a large metal object with a rubber strip doorway and a conveyor belt floor, like the thing at the airport that checks you for guns. Except that it was enclosed, and you had to open a door at the other end to get out. It was for girls only. There was another similar shaped machine for boys, but I never found out what it was called.

At first you felt the slight electric frisson that the rubber strips created falling from your shoulders once you were properly inside. Then it was completely dark, and a whirring noise began, a movement of currents of air, and you came out the other end with curled hair and frills on your blouse collar or the hem of your sleeves. Most girls were put through and the effects lasted for about a term.

Every Monday after assembly I was taken with a few others to the machine and topped up. By Friday I was back to normal, my frills having worn off. On Mondays the Deputy would eye me, me and a few mates, and dutifully, resentfully, with a shrinking substantiality, we'd walk single file to the machine and go in. Once they added a special liquid to the workings and we were blonde for a year. Old men pawed us, the boys took an interest in us, our fathers called us their little darlings.

Another time when I was raptly watching the teacher, whose mouth when she taught us our tables was pouched as if made for a kiss, I was sent to the machine and it overreacted. In the shade under the pepper trees afterwards, I noticed my arms had levers of curled-up skin. It didn't hurt, it just looked really different, like the white paper cutlet frills on a roast rack of lamb, all down my arms. I went straight home and my mother told me to wear long sleeves. During lessons I would press through the cotton, bending the skin back into place, but it sprang up again. Much later the flaps subsided, and the skin rejoined quietly overnight to muscle again. These are the faint markings on my arms.

Susan Hampton lives between Sydney and a small farm in Victoria. Five sheep, five chooks. Her book Surly Girls *won the Steele Rudd award for short fiction in 1990. Her previous books were mostly poetry. She is now working on a novel,* Nike, *to be published by Collins A&R.*

Passing

MUM WAS worried 'cause Effie was walking 'round town in a plain paper envelope addressed To the Big City.

The final geographic re-location was
soaked in blue-grey farewells
and you knew you would be going,
dying to leave me in this flat dry empty
without a picture postcard.
Dying and leaving me to read the night sky alone.

Later they said they should never have left her alone with those women singing gender non-specific love-songs on the radio. But that was before they knew and every Sunday Mum and Stella and Aunty Minna would go down to Albury, smiling, to sing in church. Then they would leave Effie with the radio-women to mind the shop.

They would watch you leave by the gardenias
at the back-gate, laughing at superstition
behind the cold creases of their hands.
They said it was the village, that you could never
leave by the door through which you had entered.
But I knew it was for the gardenias, each leave-taking
a dark-scented new entrance.

And Effie hummed as she wiped the tables and polished blue Olympia cut into the floor. She hummed as she poured the milkshakes and watched the breeze flap against the razor ribboned fly-screen through which she passed anglo, passed straight. She hummed onto the still heat of summer on the street as she went to get the Sunday papers, pausing occasionally to stand and, with her back to the sun, watch the pattern of ribboned light cast onto the pavement below.

I have never kissed a coffin before. Too late
to reconsider. My turn and the line too long,
pressing close, not to bend and touch the smooth,

dry surface. It is hot. They are impatient
but respectful — there is time for farewell, but
the words divide horizontally, seem to evaporate,
and I am left speechless.

Effie wanted to go to the Big City to hear the singing. But she knew they wouldn't understand, so she said it was the sea she had to taste before she turned twenty, with or without a husband. Only she didn't say it, she left a note so they wouldn't overload her skateboard with cardigans against the cool sea-breeze.

I cannot make a language of good evenings,
easter greetings, half-remembered lullabies.
I can no longer find the island where we stood
so many times, holding heart-shaped stones
on Aphrodite's shore.

So that night, under the crescent moon, Effie tore out of Tarcutta on her skateboard and had many adventures along the way. She may even have seen a couple and certainly, glancing up, there was a sign on the back of an old corrugated water-tank, reminding everyone they're everywhere. Effie skated by the railway-tracks, humming a song her grandmother had carried there in 1927 — carried for company, from island to continent to small country-town — wind from the turquoise sea song, red with poppies, grapes heavy on the vine, pulled from the heart album in the harsh light of the flat dry empty. So Effie continued, skating and humming under the crescent moon, looking forward to joining in the singing.

And in the Big City Effie stood on the promenade and knew the salty taste of the salty sea-breeze and saw the ocean and the ocean and the ocean, blue and green and grey. She stood by the bar where the women came together after many days passing anglo, passing straight, came together to pass out.

And Effie loved and was loved. And sometimes she sends picture postcards of the beach and writes of the music, and the women still arriving on skateboards, some with helmets, all waiting for singing to begin, waiting for the singing, for the song.

ELENI PRINEAS was born in 1962. Then, in 1986, she joined a lesbian soccer team (the Crones) after which she had purpose, identity, and something to write about. Her first story was published in Cargo magazine (BlackWattle), her next in Finding the Lesbians (Crossing), and her latest piece will be published in ITA magazine (I'm not kidding) later this year. In 1991 she visited Kythera, the Greek island where both her grandmother and Aphrodite were born, and found heart-shaped stones on the beach there (see story).

MARGARET BRADSTOCK

The Velvet Bikie
(or Life Before Solidarity)

R O Y   A N D   Phil are already there when Megan swings into the Racecourse. Roy is tall and stooping, Phil shorter and thickset, a swimmer. They are her best students and good friends. She's wearing tight jeans and a short leather jacket. Very cool. Roy and Phil call her 'the velvet bikie' — tough, but soft inside. Her ex-husband once bought her a 250cc. Honda, but she couldn't make it stand upright. It kept falling over, pinning her to the kerb; so she sold the bike and kept the gear.

Last day of term and the rest of the staff are ranged around a table in the beer-garden, ordering drinks and steak sandwiches. The men drink beer. Megan orders schooners too, determined to be one of them. Soon Janie appears, and they're suitably appreciative.

"Who's your friend?" asks Mick, who looks as though he cuts his own hair and sleeps in his clothes. "I remember her face as a student, but I don't know her name."

Mick has a reputation as a womaniser. Someone once walked in on him removing a student's bra. Megan introduces them. Janie is shy, though, conscious of her ex-student status and doesn't really join in. Some of the women ask her what she's doing these days, but she doesn't want to tell them she's on the dole. Maybe she'll come back next year and complete her Honours degree.

Megan goes off to get a round of drinks. She is gone a long time because the barman asks about the butterfly motif on her shirt. Papillon. Poor butterfly. She hasn't read the book, but she's just drunk enough to engage in a light conversation about it.

"You were gone a long time," says Janie accusingly. She seems ill at ease. Somehow, this isn't working out well at all.

Then the boys want a game of pool, and Megan agrees, knowing nothing about how to play. "Right," she says, and sails into it, sinking the black straight off. "You've finished the game," they say gloomily, starting another. "You're not meant to sink the black." Janie treats it more seriously, bending over the table with her bottom perched in the air, wiggling slightly, taking a long time to line up.

"Your friend's got great nipples," Phil and Roy comment, poking Megan and laughing to each other. She pretends to be displeased, but isn't. Faye joins them, a mature-age student with stiffly lacquered hair and a red

41

nose like a beacon. She plays pool well, but they don't appreciate it.

"Her nose distracts me," says Phil. "I keep thinking it's the ball."

"You're bastards," says Megan, laughing.

Then she notices that Janie is missing from the game, talking to a service-station attendant in a grey uniform over near the door. Megan adopts an unpossessive stance, keeping her distance, talking to the boys.

"We're going to dinner, now," Roy suddenly decides. "Why don't you get Janie and come with us?" The staff have all long gone, except for an ageing Professor, who has Faye cornered in the hall outside the women's toilets.

"You have a neck like a Doric column," he is saying.

Now she has a legitimate excuse, Megan approaches Janie and suggests leaving. "Not yet," says Janie. "This is Rex. He reminds me of my brother. I like mature men." Rex looks pleased and explains the intricacies of his business, which he manages. Megan shakes her head to the boys and decides to wait it out. Rex suggests moving round to the bar and she follows, though dinner seems a much more attractive proposition. She insists on paying for her own drinks.

"We'll be at the spaghetti bar, if you change your mind," Phil calls out.

"I'll try to make it."

Janie is drinking something white, which Rex keeps replenishing for her in a proprietorial sort of way. She doesn't know what it is, but says it tastes nice. Megan stays close. "You want to watch it. You're getting very drunk."

"Don't tell me what to do," Janie flares. Her hair stands out around her head fiercely, like an aureole. "I can look after myself."

"Look," says Rex, "I fancy her. I don't fancy you. That's the way it is. Okay?"

"Okay," says Megan. "I don't need you to fancy me. Do you understand?"

"I'd like to," says Rex, smelling slightly of sweat. "But I don't. Sorry about that. That's the way it is."

She can't get through to him. His self-confidence is like a strong wind. He thinks he's talking about chemistry, when it's a very basic preference for a younger, more malleable and nubile woman. And who asked him to make a choice, anyway? He can't seem to get that through his arrogant head with its neatly-clipped businessman's mustache and apoplectic complexion.

His friend has 'Up Kazaly' written on his shirt and comes over to talk to Megan. His friend is younger, and very ocker.

"Why don't you leave them alone," he says, after some preliminary banter. "Let them be."

"I came with her. I have to see her home."

"You're bent," says Up Kazaly. "Bent as a two-bob watch."

"And what if I am?"

He drains his glass and goes back to his mates. He's run out of cliches, and doesn't have any response to this.

"I have to go soon," Megan says to Janie. "Don't you want any dinner?"

"You don't love me." Janie's face crumples suddenly, sodden with too much drink. "If you did, you wouldn't be going to England, to Leah. If you loved me you'd stay with me, without any promises." She turns away.

Megan shrugs helplessly and goes outside. She's tempted to go home, but it's a matter of honour now. This Rex mustn't win. The juke-box is playing 'Bright Eyes' and the moon, through a haze of alcohol and tears, is huge and full. Watership Down. She thinks of Leah, of her eyes, and her heart detonates in her chest. Megan sits on the bumper-bar of her van to wait.

Presently they go by, without noticing her, and she hears the slamming of a car door. There's a metal bar in the back of the van and she fantasises about getting it, and hitting him over the head. Often, when she's drunk, she translates thought into action, all the old inhibitions gone. But she might kill him, and wind up in prison instead of England. She can see the headlines.

Instead, she goes to the car the two dark shapes are locked together in. There's the sound of a zip unfastening. Megan opens the driver's door and punches Rex in the head, as hard as she can. Dazed, he grips her around the throat, choking her. She imagines different headlines. Woman found strangled in car-park. Finally, he stops.

"You shouldn't have done that," he says."I could have killed you."

"If that's what you want to do, go ahead. What do I care?"

"I could have killed you," he repeats. "You're lucky I can restrain myself. Now leave us alone."

"Janie," Megan says, "I'm going home. If you don't come with me, that's okay. But don't bother getting in touch with me. You won't see me again."

"And if you don't come with me, you won't see me again," says Rex. Megan is tempted to laugh, but she doesn't. She waits. Janie opens the car door and gets out. She lurches unsteadily towards the van. Megan hears her own breath being expelled, slowly. Janie gets in, and laughs to herself.

"Imagine. Does he think he matters? I've known you for much longer." Rex appears at the van window and presses his card into her hand. "Here's my number, in case you change your mind." She holds it for a moment or two, absently, before it falls to the floor.

Megan drives to Janie's flat and settles her down in bed with a mug of herb tea. She'd like to stay too, but Janie is still very drunk and beginning to feel rather ill. Her sister comes in and undresses her, matter-of-factly, rolling her from side to side like an invalid.

"You rescued me," says Janie. "I'm grateful. You could have gone, but you didn't. And all those drinks he was pushing onto me. What a shit." Her face is grave, absolved.

Megan leaves them and begins the long drive home. Through the windscreen, the moon is strung up against the horizon like a helium balloon.

Margaret Bradstock published her first poem (in The Age*) at the age of five, after discovering that many interesting words rhyme with 'mumps'. Since then, she has experimented with all kinds of writing, from biography to detective fiction, and displays a rare talent for shopping lists. Her work has appeared in literary journals and anthologies, and she has read on ABC Radio, at Harold Park and other venues in Sydney and Adelaide. Margaret has collaborated with Louise Wakeling in the production of five books (including the ground-breaking* Edge City on Two Different Plans *and* Words from the Same Heart*) and recently published her second collection of poetry,* Flight of Koalas *with BlackWattle Press.*

Margaret spent her formative years in pubs and beer-gardens, has travelled widely in Europe and Asia (she can no longer, in all conscience, wear her Mao hat), and currently lives in a household overrun with children and cockroaches. Her ambition is to be superannuated.

KATE O'NEILL

Miss Cox and Me

C O M I N G   D O W N to live in Thebarton was a shock. You wonder how people can live like that, all squashed up together and noisy and smelly. I'd come from Karoonda, from a wheat farm in the Mallee with my cat, Oy. He hated it, too. His fur went slack and gritty and he started to smell funny. In the end he got not to mind it too much. He started helling around with all the other cats and running around on roofs and having fights. We weren't proper friends anymore, though, and that made it worse. Well, there was nowhere to go together. He'd land on my bed all hours of night and purr a lot and that helped. I had a bed on the front verandah, which made it easy for him to get to me. That was the best bit.

I was on the front verandah because there wasn't any room inside. That was real luck because I wasn't stuck inside trying to breathe and trying to keep out of everyone's way. They left me alone there, and people walking along the footpath couldn't see me because there was a canvas blind down. It was fun in a way because they were near enough to touch, and you could hear every word they said and they didn't know anyone was there. You could even go for walks when everyone was asleep. The night-time got to be quite good fun. What I hated was the daytime because I had to get on with people and I didn't know how.

My Karoonda grandmother was a bit of a bastard but we got on OK. She said I was someone intelligent to talk to, but then there wasn't anyone else except Grandpa. He was always limping around trying to get attention. In the end he got lucky and was REALLY ill and he could make Grandma send me away so she could spend all her time on him. I bet he thought he'd won a big victory. I'd call it living dangerously. I would have liked to be able to leave Oy there, but Grandpa put the lid on that by deciding to be allergic. Just to Oy, of course. If he had decided to get allergic to Grandma's cat she would have put HIM out of the house.

Aunty Floss and Uncle Bill were all right. They didn't have to take me and they acted as if it wasn't any bother, which it must have been. Their kids were littler than me and mainly stayed out of my way. Aunty Floss was never nasty and always did what people wanted. If they didn't want anything she sat down and listened to the wireless. She wore fluffy slippers and liked going with the kids to the matinee picture show.

Uncle Bill brooded a lot. He'd been to the war and seen Australian soldiers do all sorts of atrocities to the Japanese prisoners and he couldn't stand it. He was always picking on Aunty Floss and calling her a slut. Aunty Floss said he didn't mean to be awful, but he could have fooled me. Sticking around the house was dreary. There wasn't anything to say and there wasn't a single book. Aunty Floss said school would start soon and I'd have lots of kids to play with. I can't really stand playing with other kids. If you start winning they just change all the rules. Oy and I used to have terrific games climbing trees and pouncing around in the quarry and hunting. I just wished Grandpa would hurry up and drop dead so I could go home.

Anyhow, school started and I went along and saw Miss Cox and I knew everything was going to be all right.

You can't get teachers like Miss Cox anymore. She was probably the last one ever at Thebarton Primary school. I'd had one like her before when I was a little kid at Stirling East before I went to stay at Grandma's. They've got nice faces like horses and the only thing they want to do in the world is teach kids and look after them properly and make them safe. Miss Donahue at Stirling East had been a lot smaller than Miss Cox and not so wild, but you probably need the stronger sort when you get to grade seven.

Miss Cox was boss of the yard and used to take assemblies and she'd tear around yelling at kids and making them really scared. All the kids who weren't in her class thought she was a horrible old hag, which was good. It was like having your own private dragon.

Miss Cox was really splendid and exciting. She used to have terrific adventures, like riding camels and climbing pyramids and shaking hands with royalty and actually seeing real poets, and she did all those things just so she could teach us better when it was geography or English or art. Sometimes lessons turned out a bit odd, but she was always trying to make every one of us good and clever. It is lovely to have so much bother taken.

I felt really good in Miss Cox's class. It wasn't just because she took a lot of bother, it was because I already knew how to manage her as well. I found out all the tricks that used to work on Miss Donahue also worked on Miss Cox.

For instance, if you waved your hand around madly and grunted with eagerness you were quite safe from being asked a question. If you WANTED to be asked all you needed to do was to look as if maybe you didn't know but you had decided to be brave and give it a try.

Mainly, though, you could work it so that in no time you were having a lovely peaceful life doing exactly what you wanted. You just zipped through any work that was set and then got out a book you wanted to read or started drawing pictures. For a while you'd get pounced on, but they noticed that you always had everything done and it was no skin off their nose, so they'd let you be. Because they were so strict, kids never dared muck around, so there you were, day after day, sitting there in peace and quiet pleasing yourself and being safe from attack.

Kids not in the class would say, "Wouldn't you rather be in Miss Jeffs' class?" She was quite pretty and she had a soft voice and a nice smile and she was modern, but no, thanks. Once I was in Miss Jeffs' class for a whole day and you couldn't concentrate on anything of your own. Other kids were always sticking their bibs in.

Another thing was that you could always tell who Miss Cox liked and who she didn't like. She was extra keen on being fair, so that if she ever did like one kid more than another she'd be harder on that kid to balance out. And of course, if she ever found herself NOT liking someone she used to feel so guilty she would fall over herself being nice to them. All the kids used to think that Dula Apostoledes was Miss Cox's pet because she would make such a fuss of her and never be cross. It was lucky that Dula Apostoledes thought so too, poor bugger. Dula was a fantastically beautiful Greek girl who couldn't even pass up a book without posing gracefully to do it. I sort of hoped that Miss Cox was sorry for Dula but she wasn't. She really didn't like her.

It wasn't long before Miss Cox started treating me more strictly than anyone else. That made me feel pretty good. By halfway through the year she was almost hounding me. Kids used to say, "She's sure got it in for you, the old bag. I bet you hate her." But I kept my trap shut. Explaining anything would have been giving away her secrets.

As time went on I had to start giving her reasons for picking on me. She couldn't easily go on telling me off if I kept on behaving myself, so I got to feeding her dribs and drabs. It meant that I had to get more sociable, which was a pain. I LIKED not talking to anyone.

Miss Cox was really ugly. She looked like a witch. She had a big, craggy face with deep lines crisscrossed all over, and lots of moles and warts. Her hair was coarse and grey and it frizzed out of her bun and stuck out everywhere. She was big and clumsy and walked like a sailor just off a ship. I don't think I've seen anyone uglier than Miss Cox. It didn't seem to worry her at all. She just went on having a good time teaching us all the things we needed to know to get through life. What she REALLY liked best was teaching us Culture. We ended up knowing yards and yards of Tennyson and Mrs Hemans, and we could say a number of great thoughts, particularly great thoughts written by Shakespeare. We learnt how to reply properly to Royalty when they sent you an invitation, and we got shown a lot of masterpieces.

It was Miss Cox who made me decide to go in for being an art teacher. I had wanted to be a land army girl, but the war was over by then, and

Miss Cox said that there wasn't a lot of future in it. Miss Cox loved art. She'd started going to the art school once a week especially to learn things that she could teach us on Friday afternoons. She was very proud of her art lessons, which is why I had to end up working so hard at them.

Here's the first lesson she gave. She put a green apple on top of a stool on her desk and she said, "Now, look hard, everyone. What colours can you see?" Someone says, "Green." "Come on, more than that," so someone says "Yellow." "Good. What other colours?" Someone else, being silly, says "Blue," and she's very pleased and says, "Yes," so the kids come up with orange, red, pink, purple and whatever, and she looks more pleased and says "Yes," to the lot. Soon everyone grinds to a halt, puzzled. Then she says, just shining with happiness, "All those colours are there because colours *reflect* everywhere, so there isn't anything that is just one colour. Everything is a mixture of colours. Now, everyone, look hard at that apple and see all the colours in it, and then get out your pastels."

Well, I looked at the apple and it looked green to me, so that's how I did it, with hardly noticeable floaty bits of other colours in just to please her. Every single other kid drew an apple shape and coloured it in with stripes of all the colours they had in their box, because that is exactly what it sounded as if they were supposed to do. Miss Cox walked around look-ing, and she got more and more upset when she kept seeing stripey apples everywhere. She couldn't work out how everyone had got it all wrong. Then she saw mine and she said, "Ah, *someone* has got it right." The kids all looked at mine and they felt pretty cheesed off. If she had wanted a green apple why the hell hadn't she said so? Anyhow, she ended up asking me to go around showing everyone how to do it, so I went around at great speed whispering to them just to colour over the lot with green, and the lesson turned out OK, finally.

That is how Miss Cox got the idea that I had a future in art. Every Fri-day after that, I had the job of going around helping the other kids with their pictures after I had finished mine, so I got to be quite good at work-ing out what the hell she wanted and passing it on.

Getting near the end of the year Miss Cox started acting worried. She kept calling me out for talks about my work and getting cross. After a while it turned out that what was bothering her was that she had to work out who was going to be Dux of the whole school, and I had the most marks. It was really upsetting her. She'd probably started thinking that she must have marked my work too high all the time without noticing. Any-how, she was in a froth. She couldn't fiddle the final marks and she couldn't get over thinking she'd maybe favoured me. In the end she fiddled the bonus 'conduct' marks to make me come second. This should have smoothed everything out again, but it didn't. She probably got worried *then* that she'd diddled me out of my rightful place.

All this stewing around is probably the reason why the muck-up happened, though it was more my fault, I'd say. Well, we were both pretty stupid.

It was when she was sitting at her table marking, and the room was getting a bit buzzy as everyone started to finish off. Suddenly she looked up and said "Kathleen, stop talking," and I said, "I wasn't Miss Cox," and she said, "Don't you contradict me. Come out the front at once," so I did. Then she picked up a ruler and said, "Hold out your hand." Well, I didn't. She'd never tried to hit me before. We just stood there. There was this awful silence that went on for ages, with us staring at each other and nothing happening. In the end she said, "Go back to your seat," so I did. She went back to her table and stayed there staring at her books.

The kids had all finished their work, but they were a bit too scared to buzz much. They just sat around with nothing to go on with. Finally the bell went and she told everyone to pack up and go. When I walked past her table her eyes were fixed on her books, but there were tear tracks down her face and tears were still running.

It wasn't that I was cross about being punished for nothing. I didn't mind that at all, though I don't believe in adults hitting kids because it's bullying. But I didn't ever explain, and she might just have thought I didn't love her.

KATE O'NEILL: *Born 1933 in South Australia, thus will soon be going off the dole and onto the age pension. Live alone in small country town.*

Longtime art, drama and English teacher in Australian and New Zealand high schools. Sometime painter, playwright, actor, director, art historian, drama critic, small gallery director, book shop manager, etc.

1970s publications: one art history textbook, three one-act plays, some critical and art history journalism.

Returned from New Zealand five years ago, and have been unemployable in South Australian high schools and on the dole for half that time. It is a good life. Started writing poetry and short stories to pass the time. There wasn't much alternative; painting materials cost too much, you have to be on the spot for theatre and near a good library service for research work.

Am getting quite attached to writing poetry and short stories. One finds out somewhat more of what one actually feels and thinks, and the communication problems are absorbing. Prefer sparse, clear, accurate writing, and I enjoy the rare moments when I achieve it. Admire Chaucer's sanity, Brecht's starkness and Olga Masters' quality of every-dayness. Have no particular plans for the future. Will keep on going and see where it takes me.

1991-3 publication of short stories and poetry: Overland, Hecate, Westerly, Social Alternatives, Quadrant, Southern Review.

Ana Certiorari

Falling for Grace

MS DRUMMOYNE, new drama teacher at St Kilda's by-the-Bay, draws a deep breath as she faces the class. Seventeen girls in year 12, all wanting to be the next Judy Davis.

And one most likely will be.

Erect and poised, Grace Petrelli's body is trim and supple as a gymnast's. She fixes her Latin black eyes on Ms Drummoyne. Fiery, challenging.

Ms Dummoyne knows this inner quiver, its familiarity. This heady rush.

"Please choose your reading for the day." Her own voice, so thin suddenly.

"I thought Ms Drummoyne ... perhaps something completely different."

The class titters, hailing their woman warrior, her baits, her taunts, delivered in their languid way.

Grace lifts the book like a fan, her dark eyes all Dangerous Liaisons.

"Ms Drummoyne ... a reading from *Treachery at St Monica's*."

More giggles. A snort of laughter from the back of the room. A schoolgirls story? Circa 1938? What of Nora, Portia, Hedda Gabler?

Grace moves forward before Ms Drummoyne, the essence of supplication.

Ms Drummoyne steadies herself.

Breathing, breathing that's the thing.

> *Christmas and Miss Caldwell sent an attache case which was found to contain a tremendously lengthy coil of stout cord. Attached to it was a card bearing the inscription 'Hoping you may never be at the end of your tether.'*
>
> *Jane laughed and flushed with pleasure and closed the case, feeling a glow of something more than pride. Beth Caldwell was already the idol of the impulsive Canadian girl, who had as yet selected no special friend from amongst her school mates.*

Grace leans forward, her hand on her hip. She is Carmen, Norma, all the icons in that one gesture.

Out the window. Concentrate on the Bay. So blue. So blue.

Grace's voice, husky in the still room.

> *"Miss Caldwell, please don't speak. I am going to climb to your*

window. Don't speak and don't put on the light, but stay where you are and don't let anyone into the room."

The Queensland Umbrella tree. So Australian. Almost tropical. Never English.

Miss Caldwell had the wit to do nothing, beyond crossing to the door and noiselessly turning the key in the lock.

One flicker, one move and I'm undone.

Miss Caldwell said nothing, but she put her arm around Jane's shoulders and drew the girl close to her. She was not a demonstrative woman, but she was deeply touched by the genuine devotion of the girl.

Grace raises one hand, strokes the space before her, like a masseur skilled in Reiki.

Surely she will not touch me.

For some minutes, they sat tensely silent in the darkness; then Jane got up and crossed stealthily to the door. Miss Caldwell joined her and they stood each leaning against one side of the door frame.

Somewhere a hint of jasmine.

The light. Watch the light playing on the brickwork where the ivy grows.

Jane did not stir, but lay motionless, looking so white, but so restful that the headmistress had not the heart to waken her until the last possible moment.

"Oh, is it late? I'm so sorry. I won't be long. But I've no clothes but my riding gear."

"Yes you have, Jane. I went along to your cubicle and fetched out all you need."

The girl lowers her eyes, holding the book reverently, an actress with her script. The classroom is hushed, awed by this superb insolence.

"Hadn't I better dress in my own quarters?"

"No, Jane. Better stay here ... I think on the whole you had better stay here and keep me company."

A bird, slight with a black fan tail, hovers near the fig tree.

"Jane ... it isn't easy to tell you."

The firm mouth quivered and Jane reached her beloved friend's side at a single bound.

"Steady Jane," said the headmistress with an attempt at a smile, "or I shan't be able to tell you anything at all. And I am in real trouble this time, Jane."

Jane sank on her knees and looked up with all her heart in her honest blue eyes.

As she reads, she sinks to the floor before the drama teacher who is gazing out the window.

> The headmistress rose and came forward, and raising her hands, placed them on Jane's shoulders.

Grace takes one of Ms Drummoyne's hands in her own.

> "Child, can you forgive me?"
>
> "I, forgive you? Whatever do you mean?" stammered Jane, her face flushing and her lips quivering.
>
> "Oh my dear, my dear, my dear," was all Jane said, but she took the kind hands from her shoulder and kissed them one by one.

That night in her room, Ms Drummoyne stares into the dark. The ivy around the windows is thick and strong and the courtyard is moon quiet.

> That ridiculous girl. Why didn't I stop her?

But she must see her in the morning. Face the delicious agony of another day's class. Face all those girls and their mischievous, honeyed smiles.

She hears the tread of steps below.

> Only a tomcat, raking the tiles.

A scatter of gravel rattles against her window. Outside, the ivy shivers and she hears the familiar wine-dark voice.

"Ms Drummoyne, Ms Drummoyne. Let down your hair."

She pauses for an instant. Ms Drummoyne has the wit to do nothing, beyond crossing to the door and noiselessly turning the key in the lock.

ANA CERTIORARI is a lawyer one day a week. The rest of the time she writes, gossips on the phone, plays doppelkopf, hangs out at the pub and plans her next holiday. She lives in the future which she is always sure will be wiser, truer and more hilarious than the present. She wrote Falling for Grace at a writing group that meets on Sundays to eat, to laugh, and to write.

DIGBY DUNCAN

Spanish Hills

S HE WONDERED about the gardener. The Spanish gardener somewhere out of sight. Out of her sight, but was she out of his sight, lying there naked, her body slowly turning from its newly acquired English winter white.

She'd never seen the gardener; but Gordon had said he was there. Gordon, the blast from the past she had run into in the London pub: well more a cool breeze from a distant continent. She had first met him in Australia, a flatmate's friend, bringing English know-how to the colonies. He'd been more than a casual friend but never a lover. And now here she was in his Spanish house, far away from the London grey and a self absorbed girlfriend.

Somehow Jill's self absorption did not glow in the bright Australian light but in London it was a beacon. She had come to London to be with Jill after a stormy on/off relationship of a few years. But she had also come to see the world. These two endeavours proved incompatible.

Jill had convinced her she had seen a way their relationship could work: convinced her with phone calls and letters and promises of grown up love that could survive. She was still too much in love to throw away the chance. She knew that she would do it, she was compelled, but already she could taste the sourness of regret.

She had arrived in London in the early seventies hesitantly leaving Sydney and the sixties 'love and light' behind her. She found Jill embroiled in a tightly knit group who enjoyed seemingly mindless intrigue. They indicated that membership had to be earned but she didn't even ask the price, preferring to set up her relationship with Jill outside the group. They tagged her aloof.

After a few pints in the pub she had warmed to Gordon. In no time she was promising to paint his swimming pool and lime wash his house in Spain in return for a few weeks in the sun. She remembered what she liked about him; his unfamiliar lifestyle, his hint of mystery, and she had never been to Spain.

Jill had said she'd come when she finished the final draft of her book. But that was something to say on parting.

She'd made sure Gordon knew about Jill. Not all. Not in so many words. But she knew he knew. She wanted to think he knew.

Gordon hadn't seemed particularly glad to see her when she arrived. She had chosen to ignore this and concentrated on her own excitement on being somewhere foreign and sunny — so she was taken aback when he told her without emotion that his guests usually shared his bed. She thought he probably didn't have too many guests. She said she would sleep on the lounge. Later he managed to find a cool tiled bedroom and fresh bed linen.

It was strange just the two of them living in the house. Gordon had a business in the nearby city — Spanish money; English know how. He worked for four days and then had three off. On his days off he helped her with the painting and in the late afternoon they would drive to the coast and sit in a restaurant by the water drinking wine and eating fish. He would always pay. They would never eat lunch on these days. She would wait in anticipation for him to decide the day's work had finished. She never knew why she did this. But she fancied that he knew she was waiting and savoured the power he had. That she gave him.

The days that Gordon worked she spent leisurely. Painting slowly or not at all. She would walk down the hills to the village for lunch. Past the white-washed houses with the high iron gates and the Alsatian dogs there to guard.

When the first dog pricked its ears at the sound of her footsteps crunching on the course gravel, it would set up a warning. A chain reaction of barking would taunt her as she walked. She had a fear of dogs from a childhood in the country where untended dogs roamed in packs.

So many of these houses were locked up, shutters closed. Owned by the rich from the North of Europe, Gordon said. The rich who came only in the summers. Who feeds their dogs? The Spanish gardeners, Gordon said.

What were these dogs guarding? Women, children, property? From the gipsies, Gordon said.

She would eat a lunch of bread and cheese and wine in the workmen's cafe on the outskirts of the village. No-one spoke to her there; the owner and the old men sitting drinking coffee nodded, and after her second visit the owner just put the food in front of her; always the same thing she had first ordered by pointing.

In the market she would study the merchandise carefully but would only buy enough for the evening meal mindful of the struggle back up the hills in the midday heat. She would buy oranges, cheese, a fillet of veal or venison which Gordon liked to cook, over the open fire, for his evening meal. After he had eaten his supper they went to a bar by the sea late at night. Here they would talk and laugh with Gordon's American friends. It was an American friend who told her about Isobel and Gordon's relationship.

On the days that Gordon worked he arrived home late in the evening. When darkness fell she would sit reading and talking to the dogs, an ear out for the gipsies. Gordon had dogs too although his possessions were few.

These dogs had terrified her too at first. But it was a terror she could not afford. With tid-bits of Gordon's veal she won their affection.

When she asked Gordon about Isobel he told her that she and her child had gone back to Holland to nurse a sick mother. He said he didn't know if she would come back. He said he missed the child. Was this why Gordon was so joyless? Struggling hard not to be sad?

The warm sunny days began to meld. She began to thaw out. The cold of London left her limbs. The light, the air, the textures began to enthral her. She began tentative letters to Jill, encouraging her to Spain. She fantasized being with her here in this foreign land; of eating fish and drinking wine and going down to the sea to swim.

If only Jill would take a break, stop and live life instead of creating it on paper. But that was a problem between them. A different idea of pleasure.

Gordon had said that Isobel was obsessed with order and cleanliness, like all the Dutch, and it drove him mad; so she made no attempt at cleaning for several weeks. Then she just did bits and pieces, not too thoroughly and not too often, for her own sense of order; not enough for Gordon to notice though.

It was when she was cleaning that she opened a cupboard and the clothes came tumbling out; bold, bright colours. A woman's clothes, a child's clothes. She investigated and found still more things, personal belongings of a woman, in the cupboards high up in the wardrobe. Dirty underclothes, contraceptive pills, condoms, what appeared to be old family photos, a baby's bottle and prescription medicine for a child. There was something curious and disturbing about these objects. She looked at them for a long time trying to imagine the circumstances under which they were placed there. A shudder ran through her; she realised that the afternoon sun had gone and the cold air of the evening had engulfed her.

Gordon's American friends loved parties. They threw them often in the enormous mud brick house at the top of their mountain where the purity of the air hurt your nostrils and you could see in the distance the light sparkling on the sea like crystals. Wine and dope were mixed into a potent punch and served from a huge earthenware jar. They danced and frolicked and she joined in with zest; hungry for adventure. Gordon looked absently at home there; not uncomfortable but not there either. Once when he wanted to leave, she couldn't stop dancing. He insisted that it should be he who would take her home; so he waited. She began to feel his detached grip.

It was at one of these parties that she learnt about the infamous fight that Gordon and Isobel had had in the bar by the sea. About how Isobel had left suddenly after that. How no one had heard from her since.

She did not want to think about this ... about what could have happened but she became obsessed with apprehension. She asked Gordon when Isobel would be coming back. At first he was silent as he slowly turned the large piece of meat over the fire. Quietly he said he didn't know. Less quietly he said he didn't care. Raising his voice he said Isobel talked too much. Her talking drove him mad, he almost shouted.

She was shaken by his tone; she suggested they go to the bar by the sea that night. He was sullen and refused to go with her; so she took off alone down the darkened hills, past the howling dogs. As she neared the bar he pulled up in his car, said he had changed his mind.

She made enquiries in the bar about Isobel. The Americans knew only as much as she did; they also had their suspicions and fears. They offered her a lift to Madrid the next day.

She slept fitfully that night; only sleeping properly when Gordon left the house early for work.

She woke up debating with herself about Madrid. Was it possible? Would her money stretch that far? She got up and was engrossed in working out the costs when she heard a motorbike.

The postman rode a motorbike! It must be for her; nothing ever came for Gordon! Maybe Jill was coming after all. She felt a flood of relief.

The postman made his way slowly up the hill. Her anticipation heightened. The bike spluttered and came to a stop; he got off his bike and started to push, sweating in his full postal uniform. She ran down the hill to meet him and he handed her two letters; one for her and one for Gordon.

Hers was from Jill; Gordon's from Isobel. Isobel! She went weak from relief. Isobel alive! Not stuffed down some drain with her child.

She was aware of the postman staring at her catching his breath. She looked at his red face and felt responsible; with hand gestures she invited him into the house to have a drink. He smiled a cheeky grin, she had a moment of panic; but he refused. With fortitude he pushed his bike to the top of the hill, mounted, then sailed down to the next letter box, whistling.

She ripped open the letter from Jill and read the first few lines; Jill would not make the journey to join her: she was going to Cornwall — to think. Her energy drained and her throat hurt as she stood staring at the letter. What did this mean? Her fantasies dissolved; they would not be in Spain together, they would not marvel at the world together, make memories together. It was one of those moments when she didn't know what to do next; she slumped to the ground and finished reading the letter.

Jill said: You probably know I was devastated when you left. All I could

56

do was write — rubbish. Now I am just confused and I can't even do that. Why do you always run when the going gets rough and why do I always believe you are gone forever? How can we ever sort things out if you just up and leave for a better life, and I am too proud, or perverse, or emotionally unable to say I am terrified that I will not see you again? Will I force my own predictions to come true this time?

She heard the car arrive but didn't take it in as she stared into the empty swimming pool trying to take in the contents of the letter. The dogs barked as footsteps hit the gravel. The gipsies, she thought and got to her feet.

It was one of the Americans. He had come to take her to Madrid.

She wrote a note to Gordon — polite and thankful. She apologised for not finishing the painting. She placed the letter where he would see it and then remembered the one from Isobel — and smiled. She retrieved it from where she had dropped it, by the swimming pool.

She packed carefully but ended up with more luggage than she had come with; gifts for Jill … She stared at them then and left them in the corner of the room.

The VW van full of people edged slowly down the hills; the driver carefully using the gears to save the worn brakes. The dogs welcomed the disturbance and set up their barking chorus rounds. She looked out past the big white houses to the olive groves beyond and wondered what Gordon would make of her leaving. Would he be furious? … or relieved? — maybe neither — who knew what Gordon thought or felt and what darkness … or light was locked inside? His hint of mystery was no longer intriguing.

They drove past the workmen's cafe and through the village past the badly built modern buildings which looked like they might fall at any moment. They headed out of town.

It was then that she asked them to drop her at the airport. They agreed, amicably, and asked no questions. She simply said she had to get to Cornwall as soon as possible.

DIGBY DUNCAN: I was born in a country town, felt I had landed in the wrong landscape, felt different, had different dreams, thought it was a stage, felt lonely. Left school, tried to fit in, made my debut, drank a lot, didn't get engaged. Took driving lessons, got friendly with my instructress who charmed me with tales of lesbian life in the city. Took ages to learn to drive; she left and I wasted no time in getting to the city.

Became an accountant, lived in Sydney in the high sixties, travelled, became a filmmaker, became a feminist, unbecame an accountant. Becoming a short story writer.

The story Spanish Hills came out of my work in a women's writing group which meets some Sundays to eat a lot, write a little, read, talk and laugh together.

Among the films and videos I have made is the gay and lesbian documentary film Witches & Faggots, Dykes & Poofters and the lesbian drama On Guard.

I am interested in dreams and dreaming.

At present I am a carer for my mother who is a stroke victim. This is the hardest job I have ever undertaken.

JENNI NIXON

Marbled Effect

Spring.   Spring is young lovers kissing in the park.
Gifts of flowers,   is blue skies   not grey,   pretty frocks and ankles.
Spring   is sexual appetite.   Randy tomcats   is noisy catfights.
Flowers in bloom   is hayfever.   Swimsuits   is cellulite.
End of winter   is unfit and overweight.

I have to celebrate! Sober and six years off the smokes! Six years without a stench, burnt holes in clothes, or bedding, a fire hazard with reduced libido. Now, have feelings without reaching for a smoke screen, six years saving money, better health, breathing air. No brown tar cough, hoarse red raw throat, bird-cage brain.

I'm told, "you must spend at least $25 on yourself today, think of what you've saved!" I'd a five pack of rolly tobacco a fortnight minimum habit. A compilation of Lauren Bacall, Bette Davis, and the Marlboro Man! Sophisticated Cool! Cultivating finger tan, brown stains equal tough creative anxiety.

Buy a CD to add to my collection? Nigel Kennedy playing the Bruch violin concerto? I've only one other CD and no player, so perhaps a book? Nup, I've decided on a sex toy! It's Spring!

I send away for 'Great Sensations, Pleasurable Gifts for Women', a mail order catalogue from Fitzroy, and a little lavender book arrived with pictures and prices. Such excitement and so difficult to decide. The overnight traveller's kit with silver lady finger? The discreet Lady's Secret or a Glow in the Dark? Turtles? Butterflies? Nipple Clamps? Ouch! Indecision.

I go for the personal approach. I ring the Toolbox ... Toolshed .... Whatever! The Ultimate Adult boutique, gay and lesbian, and yes, they sell vibrators.

In my winter overcoat, Spring is hidden, have I joined the raincoat brigade I wonder, as I approach the salesman. Around me, manikins pose in edible undies, or in the leather look, there are books, comics, condoms, and things ... I'm not sure I want to know what! I know this guy who is just leaving, but I act the adult and ignore him and the merchandise. I march straight to the counter.

Gay guys are buying condoms with relaxed nonchalance. I attempt adopting the same attitude.

"I know what I want but not which one. I want a vibrator, approx. $25, in lavender."

He nods, takes me to a glass fronted cupboard with many multi-coloured sex toys, plastic penises, shiny silver balls, vibrators, all sizes in lurid colours.

"This is the lavender plain, or there is a marbled effect, same price. Which would you like?"

"Is it suitable for vaginal and clitoral stimulation?"

"I believe so."

"Marbled, I'll have the marbled effect."

"You'll need batteries, can't be returned, health regulations," briskly wrapping my new toy in pretty paper.

> Softened nipple becomes harder erect from slow
> circular teasing excitement grows anticipating
> solo sex playful with k.d. lang-uid rhythms
> accompanying gentle movement sticky finger wetness combing
pubic hair exploring massaging breathing
> alters

bells ring! impulse is ignore
pounce   responsible answer   enquiry
best telephone voice

waiting back on bed   lubricated   brightly
marbled plastic penile persuader

> surface incitement finger glow rub again and again
> harsh gulps of air thrusting faster and faster
> stabbing wetness plum ripe cum joy juice splash
> oyster pink pearl clit soaring sensations

as intrusive thoughts collide.

Do neighbours guess my new joy toy activity?
Hardly Madonna goes Shopping for Erotica!
Connecting other women   hair   eyes   mouth
lusts   those squishy obsessions   how lovely she is
heartbreaks   where is she now?   I don't want to see her anyway
ladies who lunch on other ladies
so many women use sex toys   or at least have them
'masturbation can be fun'   safe   healing

less damaging while unlearning

this not the time to muse
but how can women demand a daughter's clitoridectomy?

   waves of joyful impatience grab sighing crying grab
   and let go openings reclaiming   body   mind
   breaking taboos   fantasy journey

I put aside the sex toy not needing man or cock substitute.
Urgency returns, pleasure deepens with practice, a natural release.

Let yr juices flow!

JENNI NIXON *is a performance poet, disabled dyke, and lives in public housing, Sydney. Some of her work is published in* Cargo, *in the anthologies* Love and Death *and* The Book of the Poets on the Heath. *She has read at the Harold Park Hotel, The Edge, The Evening Star and other venues. Enjoys a wide range of writing, including escapist crime, loves the library, films, theatre, gossip, cooking, gardening, and her cat, Lucy.*

As a suicidal teenager she was shocked to read of a solitary woman stroking her nipple. Masturbation is taboo. Her father's contempt for youthful sensuality, his verbal hostility and physical violence, mocking breast buds covered by folded arms while his cock hung from droopy underpants, did not prepare her to approve a woman's casual pleasure.

FIONA MCGREGOR

Suck My Toes

FLEUR IS early. She has time to kill, but there is no bar in this quiet street, north of the city which still seems big to a Ballarat girl. Instead, Fleur takes refuge behind the paperbark tree on the nature strip and primes herself with a few gulps of tequila. She opens her pocket mirror in front of the compact, delicate, city skyline, and reapplies her lipstick.

Fleur walks down the garden path. It looks wrong, garden gnomes and neatly clipped rose bushes. The butch and femme have lived here for quite a while, and Fleur would like a better indication of this fact. Black roses, for instance, a few carnivorous plants. A cage of snakes under the fig tree wouldn't go astray. Fleur's out of a job, maybe she could offer her services as a gardener. But it's unlikely the butch and femme would pay. She'd probably just get a good spanking at the end of a hard day's work. *Ouch!*

Fleur follows the femme down the hallway, watching the hole in the bum of the femme's jeans fill with flesh, then empty, fill again, regular as a heartbeat. It's the pressure from those leather chaps hugging the femme's slim hips. Fleur would like to be wearing leather chaps too, but she couldn't get Christine's past her knees. A slow and careful dresser, Fleur hasn't much choice about what clothes to wear. Her own black jeans, white T-shirt under black leather waistcoat, brand new bike boots from Winsdor Smith. Christine's dog collar for good measure, over two smears of Chanel which don't seem to dry in tonight's heat, muggy as Sydney.

When Christine gets back from Sydney and opens her cupboard, this Chanel-scented collar will greet her like an up-yours sign from Fleur, Fleur hopes, the way Christine goes, You can wear anything you like, as long as you wash it, darling. Size thirty 501s? Oh *sure*, Christine.

The butch is sitting at the kitchen table, a foot on the chair in front, a silver skull hanging from her left ear. She'd asked Fleur to partner her in a game of pool at the AIDS benefit the other night. This is how Fleur got invited, because apart from Christine who hasn't been in this city long either, the only people Fleur knows in Melbourne are a couple of daggy cousins in Sunshine. The butch has soft brown eyes like Fleur's old dog's. She winks at Fleur, "You came!"

Fleur thinks, not yet. But she intends to, you can bet your bottom dollar. Or your top, depending on how you bed.

The butch reaches into the giant salad bowl of corn chips. Her stomach in the Safe Sex T-shirt looks loose as the hommos she scoops up with a corn chip, lolling her thighs when she leans forward, hanging slightly to one side when she leans back, elbow on the table. Fleur's stomach is big, but firm. Fleur is voluptuous fat, sexy fat, and she has perfected a walk for this figure that makes hands want to follow the curves. She does it now, around the table to the glasses, lined up on tea-towels near the sink, alternated with rows of metal cups.

Fleur feels like she's back in Ballarat in this big country kitchen — these metal cups that filled with icy GI cordial make you squeal when placed between the thighs; the long window above the long sink, and the long garden that's bound to be out there in the darkness, the yellow-white cupboards with their little round ventilator holes. Fleur's fingernails hurt over a memory of paint shards, picking it off when her mother's not looking; so thick, layer upon layer.

And the dogs underfoot. The butch and femme have two of their own, and another has arrived with a group of dykes. The kitchen slowly fills with people in denim and leather. All the dogs are bull terriers, wearing studded collars not unlike Fleur's own. Fleur's scared of bull terriers, the hard square jaws, mean and squinty eyes. She puts down her glass of water and gets herself a stubbie from the fridge.

The living room is long and sparsely furnished. A slow groove is coming from the speakers. Fleur puts her stubbie on the sideboard cluttered with aboriginal artefacts. Above is a bark painting; the constellation of dots glows like the Milky Way in the dimness. The light is coming from a fish tank the size of a baby's bath, underneath the window. Fleur watches two large goldfish glide amongst weeds a sickly luminous green. There is a rock which could be a washing-up sponge at one end of the tank. After a while Fleur realises the pale flat thing drifting behind is actually a third fish. Its snout is the widest thing on its body. It's an uncomfortable visage; the fish looks like it tried to eat some sort of bar, from the middle, and it's stuck there.

Thinking she is alone, Fleur does a few dance steps. Then she makes out two figures kissing on the couch. There's a Koori girl in a Muir cap sitting on one of the cheap vinyl chairs. She looks as nervous and alone as Fleur feels.

Fleur goes to the kitchen for another beer. She wants to save her tequila for later. Later might be at home, the way she's feeling now. This is supposed to be an S/M party, but Fleur's seen more excitement at Ballarat barbeques. Where are the whips and chains she wonders, the torture rack? The only evidence so far is the worn-out riding crop she saw on top of the fridge. Fleur is impatient for some graphic demonstrations. It seems like a lifetime that she's been waiting for those shiny, mean scenes her mind manufactures to be enacted in the rooms she lives in, parties in.

The kitchen is jammed with people, ninety percent girls. Fleur makes her way through them to the fridge. The butch is in the same chair nearby, except it's the other foot on the chair in front, and the bowl of corn chips is half empty. She's rolling a cigarette when a door on the other side of the kitchen is flung open. From beneath a mass of long red hair comes a screech, "Okay darlings, the dungeon's ready!"

The butch does a wolf-whistle. "About bloody time, Queenie."

Queenie Luckyfist is wearing the same black plastic dress she wore performing at the AIDS benefit the other night. Imported from Sydney especially for this event, it's an unexpected pleasure to see Queenie has stuck around for a few days. The dress fits her like a condom, Fleur imagines it to be slick to the touch, an oily aubergine skin. Queenie is a glistening sinew sprouting flames of hair. She walks over to the fridge with the zigzag posture that grows from her stiletto heels. "Give me a beer," she says, opening the fridge, "I'm so *sweaty*."

Fleur, arms folded, feels her own dampness spreading from her armpits. The butch's moustache is thick with sweat and corn chip crumbs. She runs her tongue along the cigarette paper, then rolls it shut, eyes probing Queenie's sleek, taut body. The femme says sourly, "You should've taken the beer from the back, Queenie, the Coronas aren't ours," then opens the fridge door in the butch's face, banging Fleur's elbow in the process. Beer spills down the inside of Fleur's waistcoat, and she moves away.

At last, someone's put dance music on. Next to the speaker is an elf-in-like girl wearing a harness and a black leather cap with a band of silver studs. She is talking loudly about dicks to a woman with a sallow, worn face and sallow, worn clothes. Dick fantasies, dildos and balls, fucking some cute gay boy. These were the people Fleur had played pool against; she hovers around them hopefully. The Koori girl hovers on the other side. The elf keeps glancing towards the kitchen as she talks.

Queenie flounces in from there. She cranks up the stereo.

                    do
                     y
PAAAAR-TY!!   *o*   (hurt me, hurt me)
                     u
                     r   *dance!*

"It's Prince!" Queenie shrieks. Hand pressed to her crotch, she dips her hips in a semis-circle. "Creeeam!"

But nobody's dancing. Except for Fleur, who begins to sway her ample hips with the grace of an African. Queenie steps from one foot to the other like a flamingo; careful in those three inch heels.

Now she notices Fleur, she smiles, she approaches. They dance op-

64

posite one another, watching bodies, feet, and the space between them begins to undulate. The space beyond them recedes. Fleur feels a runnel of sweat travel the groove of her spine, down between her buttocks. She knows her neck will be gleaming; she feels the dog collar shift and resists the urge to turn the buckle back to its proper position. It's difficult to see Queenie's real face beneath all that makeup and jewellery. A nose ring gives the impression of nostrils constantly flared; a ring embedded at the end of the eyebrow makes Fleur want to squeeze her eyes shut. False eyelashes burden the drooping eyelids and the lips have two outlines, the original one of flesh to skin, another one painted beyond this to enlarge them. The lips are encrusted with red glitter. The voice that comes from them is just as deep and rasping.

"You're gor-geous!"

Fleur blushes.

"Are you from Melbourne?"

"No."

"Didn't think so," Queenie comes closer, smiling, "They're so *cautious* here. Have I seen you around? Are you from Sydney?"

"Ballarat," says Fleur.

"Oh," Queenie takes a step backwards. "I quite like Melbourne actually," she says then, and when the song ends stands there fanning her neck. Her legs straight, slightly apart, she swivels the top of her body to check out the other people in the room. Fleur takes advantage of this moment to quickly adjust the dog collar, and get a better look at Queenie's hip-bones.

She follows Queenie into the kitchen for another beer. There's none left, only lemonade. "Oof!" Queenie leans on the butch. "I'm feeling a bit under the weather."

"Well, get over it," the butch says, "You've got work to do." She reaches for the riding crop and gives Queenie a neat crack across the backs of her thighs. Queenie bares her teeth and pokes out her arse. Fleur notices a tear in the back of the red fishnets, just behind the knee. "Get me a drink!" Queenie commands no-one in particular.

Fleur has rinsed two metal cups and acquired a half bottle of lemonade. Indicating the hip flask in her back pocket, she says to Queenie, "Tequila slammers?"

Queenie pinches Fleur's arse. "Come and *talk* to me," she grabs Fleur by the hand and leads her through to the other end of the living-room. They sit down next to the fish tank and slam the first tequila.

"Have you seen the shark?" says Queenie, licking her lips.

"What shark?" Fleur laughs derisively, thinking Queenie's making fun of her, and she'd better show she's on to it. No flies on Fleur. Her stomach twitches with nerves and all the sharp little bits she imagines Queenie would swallow with each drink, though the lips still glitter. Queenie points to the pale fish which has slid to the front of the tank, its mouth opening and closing like a long narrow eye. "That," she narrows her eyes at Fleur, "is a *shark*."

When Fleur looks more closely she sees two rows of fine sharp teeth in the fish's mouth. "Oh my God!" she looks back at Queenie, "Won't it eat the other fish?"

Queenie shrugs. The light from the tank slants across her face, around the convexity of her eyeballs, ridged by contact lenses. Green eyes, venal eyes, stare contemptuously at Fleur. Fleur pours two more slammers with shaking hands. She wants to crack through to the warmth but it is the ice in Queenie that draws her. She is aware that at all times somebody, somewhere in the room, is looking at Queenie. Fleur's under pressure. They down their slammers. Fleur watches a droplet of tequila run off Queenie's plastic-coated thigh. The border is impenetrable that encloses this foreign territory beside her. The music's getting fast and furious, a continuous ringing strings the beat together; a fire alarm, a portent of emergency, it makes Fleur feel insane. This is a nightmare and Fleur's not going to wake up. She tries to think of something to say; after the shark story everything seems bland. She tells Queenie she's staying at Christine McCaughey's, does Queenie know her?

"No," is the reply, but Queenie's already remembering the time she cruised Christine, and got knocked back. Christine's so *superior*. Bitch doesn't know what she's missing out on.

"She really fucked me around," says Fleur, wearily, "Same old story," although to Fleur it's a fairly new one, Christine being her first girlfriend. Queenie raises her eyebrows, "Well, why are you staying with her then?"

"She's not there. She's gone up to Sydney because a friend of her's is dying of AIDS," Fleur looks mournfully at Queenie. Queenie would know all about this sort of thing.

Queenie says, "Have you got a cigarette? ... What's your name again?"

"Fleur. I don't smoke."

Queenie's eyeing the elf who's smoking and sending sidelong snakey looks this way. She gets up and totters over to her. She puts her hand in the small of the elf's back. The elf extracts a Stuyvesant and lights it for Queenie. Fleur has another tequila slammer to fill the loss. Then Queenie comes back to the couch, the elf lancing a look over her shoulder at Fleur. Now Fleur's back in the hot seat she feels invincible; she glares back at the elf, expertly.

"Fleur," Queenie blows. "You need to be de-fleured."

Fleur giggles. Spirals of red hair tickle her arm. Tequila slammers. The smoke-filled light from the fish tank. The butch and the Koori girl are over near the long table in a bevy of pimply girls with stiff, coloured hair and kohl-rimmed eyes. This group blurs, so Fleur moves her eyes to events closer. The elf is showing off her belt buckle to the sallow dyke. They start to kiss. As Fleur watches, their figures wobble, then double. Another slammer, a beer chaser. The figures double again. "Let's dance," says Queenie.

"Oh," Fleur whimpers, "I can't *move.*"

"Here," says Queenie.

Fleur tries to focus on the capsule Queenie has placed in her hand. It's transparent, containing what looks like sweaty jelly crystals. "What's this?" she tosses her head, "I'm not just gonna take *anything.*"

"MDA. A half," says Queenie.

Fleur promptly puts it in her mouth. She's never heard of MDA.

Queenie strokes her neck with the red tresses. Fleur wants to tell Queenie how amazing her hair is, but she has to concentrate on breathing. Gradually, the room resumes its normal proportions. Fleur watches the elf and the sallow dyke — eight, four, two.

Ah, now things are as they should be.

Queenie pulls Fleur up off the couch. They grind to the music a sluggish pulse, androgynous vocals,

I want you to do it to me … hard …

Fleur dances closer to Queenie till their thighs touch. Queenie jerks away, snarls, pouts, then shimmies close again. Fleur feels her nerve endings prickle like a layer of static beneath her skin. They half dance, half walk to the kitchen. Queenie opens the door on the other side and pulls Fleur in after her. "Welcome to my dungeon," she cackles.

It's a small room made smaller by a covering of thick black plastic on the walls. A circle of light spreads around a red reading lamp on the floor in the far corner. In the corner opposite, a black cloth is shaped by what appears to be an ironing-board, a sewing-machine, and a chair. A thick metal chain loops from the ceiling above the sling in the centre of the room.

Queenie goes over to a low table. She puts a piece of chewing gum in her mouth then one by one, she lights the candles, black yellow and red.

I wanna be ground

Into the ground

Queenie shuts the door. No more music. For a second there is just the sound of their own breathing. Queenie pops a bubble. Fleur's waistcoat drops to the floor with a heavy, wet thud. She scoops her T-shirt in folded arms, lifts, shakes out her hair, lets the T-shirt flutter onto the waistcoat.

Queenie crouches, grasping one of Fleur's knees, she jabs the back of the other. Fleur's body jerks; she grips the wall behind her for balance while Queenie takes off her boots. The candles burn higher and oil slicks ripple across the walls. A corner of plastic has come loose and Fleur sees the pattern of wallpaper peeping through, beige, filigreed; she has come to find her mother in a room full of green sunlight and the scent of rotting plums that cover the ground outside the window. Fleur is on tippy-toes by the high bed, her mother distant on the horizon of blankets. *Mu-um, mu-um.* Creases form between the eyebrows. *Please darling, leave me alone. I have a migraine.* A pain that Fleur cannot comprehend until she wakes in the dead of one night with an axe cleaving her brain. White-faced over a plastic bucket, her sister moaning *Turn off the light.*

Queenie's face rises. Fingers spiked with wicks of dry skin run beneath the elastic of Fleur's bra, to the clasp at the back. The incipient revelation of her soft white body fills Fleur with fear. The candlelight across Queenie's lips suggests imitation jewels, the paste brooches in the props box of the Ballarat Theatre Company. These glitter lips are not kissable, the tequila breath that comes from them sophisticated by sugar-free gum. Fleur wonders if the ring in Queenie's nose gets snotty, if she has to remove the eyebrow piercing to paint the eyebrow, high, arched, dark brown. Queenie unsnaps Fleur's Harley Davidson belt buckle. Her cats' eyes stare coldly from lowered lids, she yanks at the jeans. A metal button scores Fleur's thigh.

"Ow!"

Queenie takes her by the wrists. "Get in the sling."

The door opens and the butch comes in. "You said you'd wait for me, you slut," she says to Queenie. Queenie's got the flogger from the low table; she draws it through her fist so the straps join, then explode. She flicks it at the butch. "Don't getcha knickers in a twist. We haven't started yet."

Fleur seeks the shadows to hide herself. Queenie flicks the flogger at her legs, and Fleur jumps. "In the sling!" Queenie runs the flogger up the crack of Fleur's arse, laughing softly.

Fleur clambers onto the sling. It swings and she thinks she's going to break it, like the hammock in the McCaughey's Sydney harbourside garden that holds Christine like a fly in a web. Fleur, on the lawn, looks up through the chink in her hat at Christine's thighs, wondering at the diamonds of white fat pressing through the string, and that's when her heart falls from inside her. Those legs that look so slender in jeans aren't perfect after all. Later, Fleur feels the diamond striations with her tongue, but Christine pushes her away. *Not in this house.* Fleur goes outside and lies in the hammock. The rent begins under her big bum, searing up to her shoulders through the dusk chorus of kookaburras.

It's the butch who fastens the wrist restraints. The femme, the elf, the sallow dyke and the Koori girl have filed in behind her. The line of them against the wall is contained in the V of Fleur's legs when Queenie spreads them to fasten the ankle restraints. Fleur picks out the features of her audience: the long thin nose of the femme, the sallow dyke's chin, the cheekbones of the elf, the eyes of the Koori girl which have enlarged in the shadow.

The butch starts to move her hands up and down Fleur's arms, across her breasts. This is no backyard hammock, mildew-softened; the chain above glints and swings hypnotically. Fleur is secure, she closes her eyes.

With the fronds of the flogger, Queenie navigates the length of Fleur's legs. She drifts up, back down, up again. She stops at the apex of Fleur's thighs, tantalises, then drifts back down, and Fleur is in a dream forest, autumn leaves falling around her naked body. It's a fingernail now, scoring the soles of Fleur's feet, too hard to tickle, too soft to hurt. Somebody clears their throat.

Queenie's voice rises over Fleur's stomach.

"Okay, darling, what do you want?"

Fleur racks her brains.

"Suck my toes," she says.

One by one, the toes are sucked. Mmm, there's nothing Fleur likes better, except perhaps walking in the shallows of the river. Queenie uses her tongue and the soft insides of her lips. The butch has removed the dog collar and is sucking Fleur's neck; her moustache tickles the mole on Fleur's collarbone. Fleur's nipples rise and wince between fingertips. A movement of light behind her eyelids, then heat spears into her solar plexus. Fleur screams to see the red candle tilted, the string of wax shrink back up, sway, harden, while her skin begins to throb. The butch's hand is in Fleur's mouth when the yellow candle hovers, then pours. Fleur bites the hand, swallowing pain and tobacco and palm sweat. This burning pain, peeling the skin off her stomach in the bathroom at Phillip Island; the little wet bubbles of sunburn along her bikini line and the addiction dragging to skin that doesn't want to unpeel. The black wax lands, sears down to her pubic hair. The burning, the shivering, Fleur bites the hand harder, making the butch moan into her ear. It tickles. Fleur shakes her head and knocks the butch in the jaw. Something clatters to the floor and the top half of Fleur's body is once again uninhabited.

"Shit," says the butch. "My earring."

Fleur looks down the Y of her body at the estuary of wax, black red and yellow, hardening. The pool in her navel shines, still wet. Fleur feels like a Jackson Pollock painting. O Fleur! *Objet d'art, chef d'oeuvre!*

The slap of latex on skin, a wet fart. Fleur opens her eyes and sees

69

Queenie with one gloved hand on the pump pack of lube, the other palm-up beneath the spout. Queenie's hands are in pink and blue latex; up and down they wank, making a strobe of the candlelight. Queenie starts to thrust her pelvis at the pump pack. "Oh! Oh!" she cries. "Fuck me! Fuck me!"

Fleur waits patiently in the sling. The pump pack gasps; Fleur is wilting.

Queenie curls her lip. "There's practically none left!" she says to the butch, who's come around to Fleur's feet, earring-less, and with a wet finger is doing snail trails up and down the inside of Fleur's legs, making Fleur wriggle and giggle. The elf takes a couple of packets of Wet Stuff from her pocket. "Here," she gives them to Queenie, then she goes back to her position against the wall.

Queenie empties the Wet Stuff onto a dildo in a red ribbed condom, then approaches Fleur. "Move," Queenie elbows the butch aside, and accidentally drops the dildo. She goes on her knees and feels around the floor. "Shit! Now it's covered in dust, you grot, didn't you vacuum?"

You were supposed to," says the butch. "Just use your hands." The butch comes back to Fleur's head. Fleur's beginning to feel like a suckling pig. She's beginning to enjoy this, she'd partake in the feast of herself, herself, if that were possible. She laughs, so Queenie slaps her thighs, big hard horse slaps that Fleur knows will leave red handprints.

Fleur shuts up. She shuts her eyes too.

She surrenders her top half to the butch, feels her pubic hair smoothed back and lube dumped on her clitoris. Wetness meets wetness, Fleur wants to writhe, but she is too well tied. She clenches and unclenches the muscles of her buttocks, lifting them slightly so the lube oozes down and pools around her arsehole, while Queenie's hand works her.

"She's big!" Queenie coos. A chuckle ripples along the back wall. Queenie probes and Fleur finds her rhythm. *Skreek, skreek.* "Gawd love," Queenie says over Fleur's body to the butch. "How long since you've used these restraints? A bit squeaky, aren't they?"

"Any more complaints?" growls the butch. She pinches Fleur's nipples extra hard. Her hand is back in Fleur's mouth before Fleur can cry out. Now Fleur's sweat flows freely. Her back lubricated, she slides up and down on the thick black leather.

The probing changes, an animal going deeper, deeper. You would think it's the butch being fucked, the way she grunts and groans into Fleur's neck. Fleur chews the hand in her mouth, pushing and opening around the one in her other mouth. Then Queenie's hand is in, champagne cork into the bottle of Fleur's biology, and blood rushes to Fleur's head.

Fleur enters the red zone. It's high tide behind her eyelids, brain humming full volume, her insides engorged, Fleur rides the surging. Red, womb red, a tight soft space, Fleur swims out to the deep end. Her legs, chest and gut fill with a rising commotion. She spits out the butch's hand, and Queenie begins to whimper with her,

"Oh Fuck, oh! Ow! YOWWW! Cramp!"

With an almighty squelch Queenie wrenches her fist out, and Fleur holds in the scream that will provoke slapping. The afterbirth of lube and cunt juice trickles onto the sling. Queenie is shaking her slimy hand, face screwed up in pain. Fleur feels cheated and numb. She wants to put something to the dying pulse between her legs. The butch finds her skull on the floor, and comes around to the side of the sling. "That's pathetic, Queenie."

"Oh shut up, I've got RSI." Queenie unpeels the gloves and throws them into the corner.

"You call *me* a grot," the butch yells at Queenie. "You know where the bin is!"

The elf, the sallow dyke and the Koori girl leave, muttering with disappointment. That door should not be ajar while her legs are. Fleur feels the dribble go right up past her arsehole, and the tickling becomes unbearable. She feels like a beached starfish, arms and legs outstretched, and wants to be untied. But it's important not to ask.

"How do you expect me to do anything with this equipment?" Queenie is screaming, "It's shithouse!"

"Oh, so it's the equipment, is it? I thought it was RSI."

"Let's see if *you* can do any better!"

"Alright! Wanna try me out?"

"That'd be right!" the femme screams, "Why don't you two just have a good fuck. Go on! Get it over and done with!" She leaves the room, slamming the door behind her. The sheet of plastic on the back of the door flutters loose from a top corner, revealing a beer advertisement that somebody's had a go at. *For a hard-earned thirst* the caption says. The photo of the cunt is taken front-on; beneath it a face in profile, mouth open, tongue hanging out.

Fleur strains at the restraints, eyes to the ceiling, she flexes and pulls. The chains that connect the sling to the ceiling ripple like metal snakes, and the one in the centre, directly above her, ripples as though it, too, is attached to the others.

Fleur ignores the grappling that's begun between Queenie and the butch. She yanks her arms and legs, watching the chain lurch above her head. Then it's falling towards her. "Fuck!" Queenie turns, *"The chain!"*

Fleur is still.

Fleur wakes in a dim room next to a body she doesn't know. She puts a finger to the heat that sprouts above her forehead. The lump that the falling chain made is as big as a third eye. When Fleur sits up pain jags to and from the lump, as though it's a repository for her hangover and anguish.

The head on the pillow beside her wears a shadow of hair. Fleur touches it, surprised by the softness of the bristles. The head twitches around and emits a long, phlegm-racked snore. The face is young and smooth, with a ring through the nose and one through the eyebrow. When Fleur puts her face closer she can see a delicate covering of freckles. On the floor beside the bed is a black shiny thing next to what looks like a hairy red dog.

Fleur leaves Queenie and goes into the living-room. Drifting among the weeds, making O's with their mouths, the two goldfish seem harassed. They are the only ones awake in the house. Fleur opens the container of fish flakes. A pounding begins in her head, but she makes the effort to drop three pinches of food into the tank. As she turns away, the baby shark darts from behind the rock.

Fleur stands in the tub, head poking out of the shower. The hot water hurts when it hits the lump. Big pink birthmarks are splotched down her stomach.

Fleur picks the wax out of her navel. It's embedded in the top of her pubic hair, thick, hard, red yellow and black. She shampoos her pubes and reaches for the wide-toothed comb. She drags it through the froth and wax, wincing. Tonight the girls' club is open. Fleur plans to be rid of her hangover by then. She can wear Christine's Muir cap to disguise the lump. Christine gets back this afternoon, but Fleur will insist on the loan of the cap. She pictures them dressing to go out, the casual nakedness of female friends, and Fleur wearing the burns on her stomach to disguise the others Christine made inside her.

The plug-hole clots with bits of wax, a pool rises around Fleur's feet. Broken up, under water, the wax has lost its colour. Fleur stretches out a foot to dislodge the wax, and the water rushes down the drain.

Fiona McGregor is a Melbourne writer. She won the John Morrison FAW prize for a short story in 1993 and was shortlisted for the Eltham Short Story prize. Her novel Au Pair *was shortlisted for the Vogel Award in 1992 and will be published by McPhee Gribble later this year.*

CRÈME BRÛLÉE

Buying a Bra

H AV E Y O U ever decided to give up your tried and true, trusted and blue whatever and buy a new one? Go to the experts that you have revered and feared since you were fifteen?

Recently, I did just that. I had been wearing the same bra or its fac-simile for the last decade. Now that I'm approaching a more mature age but playing more sweaty games, I decided the time had come to embark on a new look, more uptight, upfront me. Instead of slopping I would slope. Instead of a burst extra tire hanging onto my middle regions, I would have a bust. Instead of slapping myself senseless with my tits on the squash courts, I would glide and tread and stride to the amazement of my Amazonian team sisters.

So I did it. I ignored my craven, lemming-like need to go to Marketown and search out my little bra shop among the cappuccinos and pizzas. I ignored my safe little excursion round the block to support myself. I started to sweat. Panic hovered around the edge of my consciousness. Vagueness waited on the side. I did it. I asked my girlfriend to go with me, into the city and, daring and baring all, go to David Jones and buy a bra.

We hovered around the racks and racks of bras like two old perverts, examining and fingering their material. We discussed their colour, texture and lack of cloth. And we decided they were all too small.

"I want that one," I said, pointing at the oldest woman behind the counter. I knew she, with decades of boobs behind her, would know what I needed. We moved closer. She knew, instantly, kindly, in that intimate matronly way, what we wanted. She asked if she could help us. With relief we confessed. "Yes. Yes. Please. Help us."

"I, um, play a lot of sport. And I ah, was wondering if you could help me find a bra, um brassiere that could ah, support me in my hour of need, as it were."

Of course she didn't say "What's a fat middle aged little toad like you doing running around at your age?" She may well have thought it, but, to her credit all she said was "Of course, Madam. Would you like to come this way?"

She led us into the Inner Sanctum. The Fitting Rooms. It felt like a Holy Convent. It didn't look like it though. Open cubicles with little curtains. The odd bra hanging languidly from a curtain rack or peeking perkily over a partition. It was comforting to know others had been where I was about to dread.

She disappeared and returned with a multitude of matronly looking things. God, had it come to this?

I looked in the mirror. Only in changing rooms can mirrors turn acceptable bodies into butchers' window displays of prize hams and rumps. It was cruel. Tears brimmed. Fortunately, the lady bearing bras arrived back.

"Right, now try these on." How did she know I was so inept at dressing myself? "Now do it up. Right. Now lean forward. That's it, lean forward and drop yourself into it. Good. Now stand up and we'll adjust the straps." I was eleven years old again and Mum was showing me what to do with my first bra. It is comforting to know the old rituals don't change.

After much lifting and dropping and hitching, she decided on three possibles for me, then we narrowed it down to one. The first one was too big, just like my mother's and she's three times bigger than me. The second was too tight. But the third one was just right. It fitted all the right bits. It curved and padded and upheld and separated. Greying locks and the three bras.

My sweating had diminished to a steady trickle and I could still breathe so I told her I would take it. Without batting an eye, she turned in my direction and asked "Will your friend be paying?" Now that's what I call savoir faire. Times have changed.

I paid at the checkout, oops counter and thanked the lady for her help. With all graciousness she smiled and said it was a pleasure. Turning to the next woman, she asked, "Can I help you, Madam?" I think Madam was a drag queen, but I couldn't be sure.

I also thanked my girlfriend profusely for guiding me through the hell that is the city, and particularly into the store of bras, where I could get the help I needed.

What I couldn't tell her, of course, was that the bra I bought was exactly the same one I buy up at Marketown.

CRÈME BRÛLÉE was born in Newcastle on Hunter, from where she escaped at the tender age of eighteen. Her physical landscape since then has included the Central Coast and Sydney as well as travel overseas in Japan, Russia, Europe and San Francisco.

Her emotional landscape has included thousands of students, hundreds of co-workers, lovers, friends, a nervous breakdown (it didn't feel like a break-out!), therapy, buying a house, a cat, a dog and finally feeling like an emotionally mature person and at last, a writer.

Previous publications have included co-editing a non-fiction book Having a Breakdown, *newspaper articles, cartoons, short stories and poetry. A recent decision to be serious about creative writing has meant that in 1993 so far, a humorous poem has been included in the Marmalade Press Anthology, and short stories have been accepted by BlackWattle Press, Redress Press and the Australian Womens' Book Review. A lesbian romance novel was co-written in 1992 and is currently being sent to publishers.*

Crème Brûlée is a member of the Australian Society of Authors, the Australian Society of Women Writers, and Bluetongues, a lesbian writers group. Her ideal life would be writing until 2am, sleeping until 11am, meeting friends for a lovely lunch, spending time in coffee lounges, then hanging about until it was time to write again.

Lyn Hughes

I'm Just a Working Class Lesbian ...

ONE DAY a cheque arrived in the mail and changed everything. I resigned and we bought a house in the mountains. They gave me a farewell barbie and a thick black wool coat when I left work. They said I was going to freeze. The house was fibro, snug as a snail's shell. We all squeezed in and finally I sat down and wrote to my mother. She wrote back and said, 'Darling Cal I think it's a wonderful idea ...' and I smiled for half a page and then she said 'And if anything happens between you and Sue at least you'll have the house as an investment.' Sue read it over my shoulder and howled. "She always thinks I'm going to leave you. You're sort of tossed on my horns, bloodied, always about to fall." Sue's turn of phrase, like her paint, spread thick and lurid.

I loved the house. I loved the garden. I'd come home. The trees were different and the birds but there were three gooseberries on a bush and a straggling raspberry cane with green shrunken fruit. I was born in South Wales in a house looking onto a forest, near the viaduct. Now I looked down onto the tops of gum trees. Months later they were top-heavy with snow. My mother used to dig us out in winter. There's a photo of her wearing something like Ug boots and a shovel. Or perhaps it's not her perhaps it's her sister. Four years after we moved in we were still fighting by airmail. She wrote, 'Don't forget your grandfather was a school teacher for forty years.' In case I thought I was better than my family. He had a real job. My other grandfather worked in the steelworks. I wasn't ashamed of them. My mother's blue eyes looked across the breakfast table out of Sue's bony face. "Why don't you just stop writing?" she said, but I couldn't.

I'd come home to the mountains. Sue had a shed in the garden, wooden slats let the light in and she painted there. Everything looked like a parrot-blur, she didn't use anything but primary colours for a year. We were both on the wing. Everyone's roof was peeling, it wasn't just us. We sank into genteel poverty. But my accent always gave me away. Sue, with her private school, talked through her nose. When she talked to the mechanic I couldn't understand her. We bought tracksuit pants and wore two pairs of socks and fleecy checked shirts from K-Mart. I didn't think I was better than anyone. The main street of Katoomba could have been Crumlin or Risca. People had thin hair, badly cut, and skin stained by cigarettes.

The first wave was just beginning to break. The Yuppies, coming over the top, wave after wave, buying things. Painting the roofs. The boys down the street leaned out of their ute and shouted "Lezzos! Are you two Lezzos?" And I shouted back. "Yes," and was terrified they'd heard me. I'd been pushed up against garage doors by boys like that, tongue kissed, dogged by boys on bikes. They couldn't have heard. It wasn't more than a whimper.

Sometimes at night I'd dream of women and sometimes men. It was a growing phase. I planted a wonga-wonga vine to hide the woodpile and it grew berserkly in all the wrong directions. I had to keep finger pruning it. And I felt like that. Are you two Lezzos? We went to a lesbian social club, to a bar, to a band. We were 'identifying'. It was more two wonga-wonga vines twisting around each other, getting in each other's hair. My mother wrote, on my birthday card, 'I'm so lost without your father I want to die.' It had a picture of cats on the front. We both loved cats. I'd always thought that my mother was a waif, a stray, and now I saw the truth, my tiger, my avaricious leopard. 'I know, I know,' I wrote back, said on the phone. I know, I thought, to begin with you never had anything. Crumlin, going here and there overseas, always looking for the better deal. Australia, South Africa. I'm just a working class lesbian. It sounded like a song, but I'd lost my voice. My mother was honing hers. 'You could have gone to University, it wasn't our fault,' she wrote. In 1958 my father worked in a cement factory in Melbourne. He pulled himself up by his bootstraps. But when I saw his feet, after he died, they were always in worn sandshoes, digging up potatoes. I couldn't imagine cement dust, covering him, he was too tall for Santa Claus, for a Welsh fairy. My father was ashamed of his mother. Did he tell me that, when he was drunk? Ashamed of her lack of education? When he was drunk we talked, he put his arm around me.

My mother wrote, 'I've always been there for you. Even your love of words was mine.' And I thought, well, we've all been peeled, segmented. We were working class, lower, middle, upper, and now I don't really know what they all mean. I looked back on our council house in Wales romantically as my hobbit-hole. A red robin came to the back garden patch each winter and I fed it. The red of a parrot. Was it the connection? Did my father grow potatoes there too, at Severn Avenue? I passed the ll-plus and went to Grammar School for seven months. Why are we all writing about it? Is it because we are orange segments who want to be put back together? Wanting to find the romance.

My mother wrote, 'You're so cruel, all I ever wanted was what was best for you. That's why I stayed with your father.' She was almost being honest. Sue said, "God, more deceit. When will they all face the truth? The women of that generation!" I was reading about a woman who went to a Grammar School and whose father was never there. My father worked shifts for 25 years and was home at unnerving hours. He would cook, iron, but he wouldn't push a pram. Was he an average working class man? His father didn't cook. His father sat in an indoor chair, placed out under an apple tree, with his knees crossed and a pipe drooping from his bottom lip. He made my father leave school at 14 and I left school at 16. Perhaps I was clinging to some sort of family solution. Work. Wages. The work ethic. My parents emigrated to Melbourne and my father worked in a cement factory, that's what there was. My mother wrote, 'I'm just waiting to die. All this money, these holidays, clothes, trifles, are nothing.' And Carolyn Steedman said the political motivation of the working class was greed, avarice, resentment. They want to be Liberal voters. Her mother wanted a coat in the 1950s 'New Look' style. My mother wanted to buy things, easily, effortlessly. She said, looking around our house, "I don't know how you can live like this." She meant voluntarily. Because they'd spent their lives trying to put it together, on HP, and later cash on the knocker. How could I choose to let go, discard the entrapments, the three-piece lounge suite? And we'd come to a crossroads, we were different people.

My mother always needed a night-light because she'd grown up with rats in the roof. Crumlin was stone, could have been Haworth Cottage, but smaller, meaner. There was a small milk-bar in Crumlin where they all went. But my illegitimate grandmother kept herself to herself. The trades people used to call on her at home. My mother always told me this with great pride. And her husband was a school teacher. These are just words. There is nothing, no black night, no moor, more gothically eternally bleak than Crumlin in winter in the rain. They scrabbled out of it, emigrating when I was four. Melbourne. "I don't know," my mother grumbled, "why they hate us so. Us English." She meant Welsh. In 1956 Melbourne wouldn't differentiate. "Uncivilised, the lot of them," she said. They gravitated to other émigrés. We kept selling up, moving on. My mother felt cheated. I don't know what my father thought. The cement works didn't last for ever.

It wasn't just the three piece lounge, it was the choice of sexuality. The choosing. "I've got a tattoo on my left breast, a heart with a dove snug inside," a woman at our lesbian club said. And that was alright. It was hidden. Like the rats in my mother's night-roof. But there was fear. What if I had a tattoo? On my wrist? Where people could see? Katherine said, "My father used to beat us. And then cry. And then we could talk. He couldn't talk otherwise." We sat in a circle and talked and listened. I felt earthed with my bum on the floor. I didn't want a chair, I didn't want any of it. Was Katherine's father as tall, as volcanic, as on-his-knees as mine?

Was this a working class man? This inability. To talk, to tell, to love? Charlie, who was square, two earrings in every flap, shorn, said, "My mother pretends she doesn't know who I am if we meet in the street." Charlie, my daughter?

My mother wrote, 'Your father was so ashamed of you. And the children, that's all we ever worried about. What would become of the children.' And I lay in Sue's arms, gored, crying. "It was different then," Sue hushed, "They couldn't choose." "They didn't want to," I sniffed and lay in the luxury of talking.

Lyn Hughes was born in South Wales in 1952. She lived in South Africa for 18 years — the setting of her first two novels. Her first, The Factory, *was published in 1991 (Pascoe Publishing) and was shortlisted for the National Book Council's 'New Writers Award'. Her second,* One Way Mirrors, *is published by Allen & Unwin (1993). Her fiction has been published in* The Babe is Wise, Cargo, Australian Short Stories, The Pink Ink Anthology, *and* BURN.

She started writing in 1983 when she joined a Women's Community Writing Group. Putting poetry into prose is her overwhelming ambition. She is currently working on her third novel, The Bright House — *a lesbian novel set in Sydney.*

Jenny Pausacker

Waiting For the Publisher

HOW IT FEELS

Tight and close, like one of those old moulded breastplates that mimic the muscles in bronze. At worst, bad for breathing.

Fine all day, nothing to say as I walk round the city, meet friends for dinner, go to bed, read. Then an hour before sleeptime I start to read at speed, and I look up from the page to find I'm tightening.

I lie down and I'm gripped by terror and I try to stop it taking words because I know, I do know, really, that they'll be the wrong words.

HOW IT STARTED

I was having a familiar argument with one of my housemates and I went and got the whiskey, and after that I found some gin. Then I was very sick. It took me a few days to trace my way back to the fact that I'd just sent nine months of novel to a publisher.

"Nah, I feel fine about it. I mean, there's only three things they can do — accept it, reject it or ask for rewrites — and I want to rewrite anyway." That's what I was telling people.

MY NOVEL

— A pile of foolscap four inches high, covered with small spiky biro marks.

— A pile of foolscap two inches high, covered with neat type inside clean margins.

— Piles of photocopies for my friends and their friends to read.

— A glossy rectangle of bound book, displayed on shelves, opening in people's hands in libraries. With a print run of two thousand, then if four people read each copy ... if four people read each copy ...

WHAT I WANTED TO SAY

That's in the book. It's even in the pile of foolscap.

Or is it? Did I say it right?

WHAT DO I MEAN BY 'RIGHT'?

Right for me. (Did I say what I meant to say, or did I play tricks on myself, like saying I felt fine and then drinking whiskey and gin?)

Right for them, the audience. (Will they all like it? Can they all like it?)

Right for the times. (There are fashions in books, too, hard to predict in advance.)

Right. (Saying the right thing, embodying the right values, the right ideology.)

Right. (Marxists and capitalists, feminists, the Festival of Light, academics, you, me and that person over there all sometimes say, "This book's better than that book. This book's got it right." Whatever it means, we all sometimes say it.)

DOES IT MATTER?
— Yes.
— No.

HOW TIME PASSED

I tried to talk about it. I tried to put it out of my mind. I worked on other jobs. I took a holiday. I went into town and bought clothes and books and a shiny black mug with pink and gold flowers. I started to train myself to eat vegetables. I planned my next novel. I planned to go away.

And the last hour of waking felt increasingly tight in the stomach — at worst, bad for breathing.

MEANWHILE, BACK AT THE PUBLISHERS

Fuck cool. I ring them.

"Some other readers. Holidays. Offices renovated. Three weeks."

"Oh, fine." (But what did you think of it? Please?)

WHAT I DID NEXT

I read George Orwell's *The Prevention of Literature:* "There is no such thing as genuinely non-political literature"/ "Whenever there is an enforced orthodoxy — or even two orthodoxies, as often happens — good writing stops."

I reread Mao Tse-Tung's *Talks at the Yenan Forum* on Literature and Art: "We oppose both works of art with a wrong political viewpoint and the tendency towards the 'poster and slogan style' which is correct in political viewpoint but lacking in artistic power."

I remembered Jean Devanny writing to Miles Franklin: "Oh Miles, how I have wasted my life. I'm done for now, yet I feel I had it in me to do good work ... I realise now that I have not exploited the small measure of ability of writing I possess one whit. I have never really got down to it and THOUGHT. Thought was reserved for politics."

I discovered Joanne Russ's *How to Suppress Women's Writing*: "In everybody's present historical situation there can be, I believe, no single centre of value and hence no absolute values ... When we all live in the same culture, then it will be time for one literature. But that is not the case now."

Three weeks later, with a much better political understanding of my dilemma, I rang the editor again. We chatted for half an hour and laughed at each other's jokes. Finally I forced myself to say, "So what are the odds? Fifty-fifty? Sixty-forty?"

The editor laughed at my joke.

FEARS
Fear of failure. Fear of success. Fear of wanting to succeed in that world. Fear of being seen to want to succeed in that world. Fear of failing to succeed in that world.

And besides, you've never had a job. You don't know a wide range of people. You're middle class. You hide away. You hold in your feelings. You worry about everything. You're uninteresting. Irrelevant.

Those were my fears.

Oh, and by the way, I ought to mention

WHAT THE BOOK WAS ABOUT
Lesbians among other things.

MY FRIENDS
Some of my best friends are writers but more of them are readers, so they don't always understand the way publishers work. Well, come to that, I couldn't actually explain to them why the whole process took so many months, why I didn't just demand to know the editor's opinion and why my union couldn't do something about it ...

All the same, I wasn't waiting for the publisher on my own. I'd passed this manuscript around, so I could use my friends' criticisms in the final draft. It was a help, having heaps of people who were interested to know how the book was going— but on the other hand, my first experience of waiting was combined with my first experience of learning to handle criticisms from those closest to me.

Scorpios have this exhausting tendency to try and tackle everything at once.

AND THEN
The week before I was to ring the editor again, I went away with Nance to relax. Relax! I could hardly breathe. In the car on the way back, we had an all-stops-out fight, and while we were still working that through, I got

up one morning to find my mail outside the bedroom door, including a big parcel from the publisher.

Since they'd returned the foolscap, they'd obviously rejected the novel, so it only remained for me to read the editor's letter and the reader's report.

The reader admired my courage in tackling the taboo topic of lesbian love in a novel for teenagers. The reader felt, however, that the book would only reinforce young girl's worries about being normal. The reader believed that older teenagers, who might find the book helpful, would not read books written specifically for teenagers. In conclusion, the reader regretted the book's lack of literary merit.

So at least I'd spent my time thinking about the right issues.

LEARNING FROM MY MISTAKES
I decide to skip the Women's Ball. I don't want to say "No, the novel was sent back" to everyone I know, all in one night. Instead I walk into town and spend money. In the empty house I admire my presents, arrange food on the best plates, watch *Starstruck* on the TV and howl my eyes out when the tough young girl wins first prize in a rock band competition.

THINGS IMPROVE
Okay, I can make plans for the second draft now. And I know a lot more about being a feminist/worker/lesbian/writer. I mean, the aim is to get to work on the contradictions, isn't it?

I sleep soundly. After a weekend of lazing, walking and catching up, I curl myself around sleepily in Nance's bed. And there's that metal breast-plate again.

Oh no. I've become a spiritual hypochondriac.

But I finally remembered that I still had to talk to the editor.

WHAT THE EDITOR SAID
The book had been sent back, so it was mine again. I sat in a coffee shop and talked as directly as you ever do when it's work. We relaxed and after a while the editor said, "It isn't the way I'd like things to be, but your book does need to be better than other books."

WHAT I DID NEXT
Started the second draft. What else?

A FANTASY
It's alright for me, I thought. I work as a writer; I'm a Scorpio; I've got lots of confidence; heaps of friends to support me; everything feminism can tell me to date. They won't suppress this woman's writing.

But I imagined a woman who was torn by the conflicting messages; who was undermined by the demand to be more than others had to be; who wavered in the balance between what she had to say and how she had to say it; who put down her pen, muttering, "If they don't want to hear it, I don't want to tell them."

I felt sorry for her, and then I realised who she was.

ANOTHER FANTASY

Sometimes I wish I was a lesbian carpenter. Or a heterosexual woman writer. Or a male writer, heterosexual or homosexual. I wish I came from the kind of minority that makes people say, "It's not your everyday experience, but it's so fascinating to read about." Or I wish I was me in my twenties, living day by day, talking to anyone I met at the kitchen table, writing a story or a play every so often, planning to write something serious one day.

Of course, it's quite probable that other people sometimes wish they were me. And in the end my book, my second draft, was published and reviewed and read. And a lesbian feminist writer in a homophobic capitalist patriarchy needs to expect to spend time waiting.

It doesn't need to be a passive activity.

Jenny Pausacker: I wrote Waiting for the Publisher *in 1984, while I was waiting for the publisher. (Kept thinking it was finished, kept needing to add another section.) For some reason the piece demanded to be written in short story form, rather than as long scrawls in my diary, though I never expected to see it in print, let alone anthologised nine years later. Then again, I'm starting to realise that my most intensely personal stories are often the ones that most people identify with ...*

Waiting for the Publisher *is about my young adult novel* What Are Ya? *which eventually won the Angus and Robertson Junior Writers Fellowship, was reviewed all around Australia and short listed for the South Australian Festival Children's Book Award and the Alan Marshall Children's Literature Award in 1988 and has been published in Germany and England. That sounds good but I have to add that it was also remaindered in 1992, after my editor (not the one in the story) told me that 'It's a pity* What Are Ya? *was before its time.'*

Meanwhile, I'm still on with Nance. I'm still writing — for kids and adults, about lesbians and teenage boys and the 1930s Depression and magic remote controls that let you Fast Forward your own life. I've switched from collective households to living on my own and I've switched from earning the main part of my living by writing educational kits to earning the main part of my living by writing teenage romances under a number of pen-names. But I still go shopping whenever I need to cheer myself up and I still keep learning from my mistakes.

MARY FALLON

The Wound & The Message

(an extract — Chapter One)

T O T O   S A I D   one drunken night — shit could that woman drink — she said, "Evie and I were like sugar and water. Can you imagine what I mean?"

I couldn't. I'm Shadowbox, friend, confidante, gay as a blade and this is how it went.

She was morose and drunk — "Like sugar and water and now when I think of her all I can see is my favourite cotton dress hanging on the line fading in the sun, faded."

It was a tragedy I didn't want to go into so I bought another round and changed the subject — not for long. She could be bad news when she'd had one too many.

"You know what she said to me? Ya wanna know what that switch bitch said after five, no six years? She left one night and all she could say was — I asked her, I said, 'Why. Why are you doing this? I love you,' I said, 'Why?' — and all she said was, 'It's nice having a nice relationship with a nice person.' I'll never forget it, never. That's what she said after six years — IT'S NICE HAVING A NICE RELATIONSHIP WITH A NICE PERSON. I never got over her saying that. I still dine in the dell dwell on it."

It was so embarrassing when Toto got like this. She COULD be such a riot. She was great at parties but you wouldn't want to live with her. Just my luck, I thought, to catch her like this.

"And yawannaknow what she says to me one day, the first day I met her after she left?"

God, there would be no stopping her now and, no, I did not want to know, not at all. She took everything so seriously. She was really obsessive. It was such a bore.

"She said — you know I was desolate, sexually desolate, I was desperate, completely fucked — and she said and, honestly she sniggered, and she said to me who had loved her faithfully for so many years, she says, 'Had any good sex lately?' Honestly. I still wake up crying hearing her saying that — HAD ANY GOOD SEX LATELY. I don't know what it means anymore, that has no meaning for me. It's like asking a cripple how she likes running in the Sydney to Bondi — NO meaning. You know what I mean?"

I didn't, thank god, but I nodded and wished I'd gone straight home after work to watch that Bette Davis movie on TV. Anything but this lot. Heaven only knows, we've all had our problems.

At this point, two women walked by arm in arm and a sort of ominous silence fell as we all wondered vaguely if and when the great fist would fall and that shut her up a bit.

"Actually," I said, "I saw a guy in a wheelchair being pushed by a friend in the last City to Surf."

"When I look back now I think she was probably trying to be frank or dick or something with me but when I asked her why she had to talk like that to me and was it her pathetic way of being honest she said — get this — she says, 'How long is it since I've been wet for you?' and all done with that pretty little pink tongue which had been so long in other places."

Oh, really, she does go too far. Why did she go on like this? I'd heard it all before. We've all had our ups and downs. It was hard enough to get by without her bloody carry-on. She thinks she's the only one to have ever been done wrong.

"Come on," I said, "I always liked Evie. I always thought she was lovely."

"So did I, you fuckwit. I still do, that's why I hate myself. How would you feel about yourself if you still loved someone who had done that to you?"

Always a fucking answer. I just wanted to get away. This was a one way trip to the pits.

"OK, people are all mongrels if that's the way you want it," I said, "but what about Freda? Aren't you happy now with her?" She just laughed and started quoting something. Well, I was off and I wasn't the only one. I certainly wouldn't be ringing her again in a hurry.

When at last I got out into William Street I noticed someone had graffitied in big black letters with a big fat brush, IT'S NICE HAVING A NICE RELATIONSHIP WITH A NICE PERSON, all over the empty, blue sky. I looked back to wave but she was mumbling away in her cups.

Mary Fallon grew up in Brisbane and moved to Sydney in her early twenties. She lived in London for a period in the seventies and in Paris briefly a decade later.

She has been writing over twenty years. In the eighties she self-published two books Explosion/Implosion *and* Sexuality of Illusion *which experimented with language using poetry and prose, and exploring the boundaries between them. Her novel* Working Hot *was published by Sybylla Press in 1989. She also wrote the text for a musical which was performed at the Bay Street Theatre. Her performance pieces include* Credibility Gulf, *a work about the Gulf War. Other works have been broadcast by ABC Radio on Background Briefing and the Coming Out Show. She is currently working on another novel and a stage piece* Matricide — the Musical.

She moved to Hobart for love, but has found she is not made of the right stuff to live in Hobart. She is going to flee to Melbourne and travel back and forth across the strait. When in Melbourne she will carry a sign: 'Warning. I've been living in Tasmania. Take Care before Entry.'

SUSAN HAWTHORNE

Meditation on Falling

W HAT IS the velocity of a falling body? a body moving through space, sensing neither the relative time, nor the relative motion of its fall.

How long does a body   falling into a seizure   take to fall?

Which is the time?
Which is the space?

If a body is senseless to the motion   the time   the space   the pull of gravity as she falls   can she be a sentient body?

If a body only notices that she has fallen   (now face down on the ground) that it happened some time before this moment   (her eyes open to her position but not to any memory)   that gravity has pulled her down — how can she know she has fallen?   that time itself has been seized?   that memory has not encoded the moment or the actualisation of the fall? What then?

If memory has for a moment   (or for several unquantifiable moments) been erased   scrubbed clean by the fall through time   through space what proof has she that she exists?

Only later, when she says   What happened?   (assuming something did) can she call on her existence.   But when she fell   sensing none of the things essential to conscious existence   did she exist as anything more than an object falling?

She can know only that she has fallen through space into another time but only as an object.   At the moment of non-existence she cannot be a subject   (except that she is subject to the laws of gravity and the continuous flow of space/time).

At the moment of non-existence during the fall   she   (like any particle) could move along one of two paths   a tendency towards non-existence (death)   in which case the subjectless state would have persisted   or she could resonate towards a tendency to exist   (which she did)   and move back towards the possibility of subjectivity.

She leaves a frail trail of light   burning brighter   as consciousness returns to her eyes.

She lives!

Fitting it Together

ANNA WAKES in a strange bed. Her mind is blank. Empty.
"Where am I?"
"Don't you know?"
"No ... I ... don't."
She scours the walls for something familiar. She does not recognise the room. A woman bends over her, half naked.
"How? ... I don't understand."
"You had a fit. Do you remember anything of last night?"
"No."
"That's a pity, it was such a good night."
"Why? What? What happened?"
The emptiness presses her back against the sheet.
"You decided to stay the night. You came to dinner and then you were too drunk to drive."
"I remember backing my car out of your drive."
"That was because it was blocking access and ... ah ... we didn't know you were staying at that point."
Some of it is emerging from the black emptiness inside her head. An image here and there that she can barely grasp.

We were lying on the floor in front of the fire, both of us drunk from too much wine.
"Do you remember what we talked about last week?"

"Yes."

"Well, it's all changed. We've decided to split up."

"Is that a you, plural, decision?"

"No, not really."

"Why do you think she wants to finish?"

"Boredom. I don't really know. I think there are things she isn't telling me. She says she wants to be celibate. Basically, she's not interested in me anymore."

"And what about you? What are you going to do?"

"Oh, there are several possibilities ... and you're one of them."

She reaches out and touches my hand lightly. I lean over and kiss her.

"I don't know about this. Isn't it a bit soon?"

"She can hardly complain."

"But what about our friendship? I think I should go home."

"I'm still too drunk."

We lie there, discussing the pros and cons of sleeping together, for two hours — occasionally touching and kissing. Her hand brushes against my breast, as if by accident. I press my tongue against her neck. We lie in a tight embrace.

"I should ring her. Or she'll worry."

"What about tomorrow?"

"I'll tell her we slept together."

"You don't have to tell her."

"Yes I do. She'd know anyway."

I go to stand up.

"Are you sure?"

"Yes, I'm sure."

I ring.

She removes her clothes. I would like time to just look at her, but she dives into bed. Her skin sags a little. Nicely. I crawl in beside her. The feel of nakedness ... it's so long, months.

"I don't know if I can remember how ..."

I realise that for her it is years. She turns to me.

"When did the possibility of sleeping with me first occur to you?"

"The first time I came here — for lunch. I can even remember what we had — parsnip snoup, I mean soup, and a prune tart. I don't remember the main course. What about you?"

"Oh, a long while ago."

Our hands move. I can feel my wetness seeping. The familiarity makes us tentative. Tongues press against lips, teeth, tongue, nipples. We murmur.

The silence is broken by breath drawn heavily through nose and mouth. From time to time we reach for water to moisten the alcohol dryness of our mouths. Cool wet kisses.

Her nipples erect to my touch. Her hair and cunt are wet. I press my legs between hers. Clutch at her cheeks. I plunge my fingers into her. Our bellies connect, like Siamese twins.

We rest.
"I don't know whether I feel adulterous or incestuous."
I am silent with my own confusion.
"I don't suppose it matters really."
"Do you think we'd be here if we hadn't been drunk?"
"No."
"And why didn't we speak of this on Tuesday?"
"Because it was daytime, and we were sober."
"Yes, that's what I thought."

We begin again.
The night draws on.
We stop and start, stop and start, I don't know how many times.
"You sex starved thing."
We begin again.
"I'm at my peak. Thirty-six. It seems a pity to miss out at such a time."
"You told me about that the day you came to talk to me about Jenny. Do you remember?"
"Yes. But I'd forgotten."
My finger runs lightly over her clitoris.
"You are good."
"I'm glad you think so."

She is sitting, in the sun, on the edge of the bed.
"Are you all right?"
"Yes. I can remember it now. I still feel disoriented though."
"I didn't know what was happening. I was too slow to put something in your mouth."
"It's not a good idea. It's better just to hold the person and allow the fit to proceed. I always bite my tongue anyway. See."
Anna stretches her tongue out to where the teeth marks are visible.

"How long did it go on for?"

"It felt like hours, but it must have been only a couple of minutes."

Thoughts struggle into place. The picture is nearly complete. Memories of pleasure sweep through her. Anna reaches for her.

Susan Hawthorne is the author of a novel, The Falling Woman *(Spinifex Press, 1992), a collection of poems,* The Language in My Tongue *published in the volume* Four New Poets *(Penguin Books, 1993) and a feminist quiz book,* The Spinifex Quiz Book: A Book of Women's Answers *(Spinifex Press, 1991/93). Her work has been widely published in magazines and anthologies. She has co/edited four anthologies:* Difference *(1985),* Moments of Desire *(1989/90, with Jenny Pausacker),* The Exploding Frangipani *(1990, with Cathie Dunsford) and* Angels of Power *(1991, with Renate Klein). In 1989 she received the Pandora Florence James Award for Outstanding Contribution to Women's Publishing. She lives in Melbourne.*

PAMELA BROWN

A Small Story

SOMETIMES A song which reminds me of you comes on the radio. It happened this morning. It was Elvis Costello singing *Too Far Gone*. I was in the kitchen, washing up. The radio is in the lounge room. I went there, sat down and listened, and I thought for a long time about you. You used to sing those kinds of songs.

I could always hear her coming. Wherever she went, she entered talking. A loud semi-monologue, half addressed to whoever she met, half to herself. I always liked this way of hers, these entrances, these brisk attacks. In those days, my room was tacked onto the back of a rambling old house. When she came to see me I would hear her talking her way down the long corridor and out through the back door. In earlier days, the best times, expectation would set off a tiny flicker in my pulse, little anticipations, and she would arrive in my doorway, with the light behind her. And we would go in her car to Neilsen Park, or Bondi, or Watson's Bay, which was probably her favourite place.

We climbed up over the safety fence and walked across the flat rocks to the cliff edge. The enormous ocean swirling and crashing against the rocks hundreds of metres below us. I said: "There are magnets down there." Magnets in the dark green swell. You sat down and murmured that I said that every time we went there and we laughed. You looked out at a ship slowly crossing the horizon, and I looked at your softly tanned shoulders cut by the line of a pale blue singlet and felt a dangerous tenderness. There was always this edge. This strange danger. It was there from the beginning, based on a certain vulnerability one which most people know of letting your feelings overpower you, losing all protection, always unsure, in love, that you are loved in return.

Daylight saving was a gift. Most of this, the days I like to remember took place in summer. A warm December afternoon, standing on her verandah looking across the park to the small bay, and further to the grey arch of the Harbour Bridge nudging the sky. We were about to drive to Neilsen Park. We had spent the afternoon in bed, and everything looked sharper, keener, the way it does when you've exhausted your senses.

We sat on towels on the sand. You wiped the tiny drops of water from your face and I noticed the freckles the summer had brought to your cheeks. You took out your tobacco and we rolled cigarettes. Long streaky shadows fell across the beach. You picked the loose bits of tobacco from the end of your cigarette. We talked the way lovers do. I can't remember our conversation, only the way it felt. I always remember the feeling of things, not what is said. And the way the sea seems to be a key to memory. To nostalgia, sentimentality ... which is the way I'm feeling writing now.

That summer I became close to a friend of yours called Val. I wonder why hardly anyone seems to write about friendship between women. Someone asked me that the other day. I'm thinking about it now because I was close to you both, loved both of you, but the kinds of love were different. Val once wrote a song for me. You sang it. It was a great song. I've never had a copy of it but I can remember a few lines:

If I touch you it doesn't mean a thing,
We can let this dance become almost anything,
I'm only reaching for the fragile and the strong,
No need to get it wrong.

This is something about the way we were together. And we were never sad together. Sometimes quiet, but never sad. Now it's as if I travelled easily through it, just kind of walked through ... like brushing someone's arm in a crowd. Val moved in to the house where I lived. We sometimes talked about you as we often talked about many other things.

On her birthday, she would take her camera to her friends' houses to photograph them. To me this seemed a serious thing to do. It probably came from her interest in history. It wasn't art. She was an archaeologist. She had done this for years.

This is a small story. The song on the radio brought it back to me. I haven't told the details. I can only say that conflict grew to be the necessary fire of our relationship. I know this happens to most people. I think it probably only happens once in one life.

There are some things which mark you. The memory fixes like indelible ink, permanent and poisonous. Sometimes it happens when you mix sex with ideas; sometimes it just happens. Each in our own way, she and I had moved so cautiously, like tigers in a cul-de-sac. I was studiously contemporary so I would seem to have emergency. She was absorbed in the nervous remembrance of history. This seemed to be our conflict. And, as women, conditioned for self-scrutiny, we monitored ourselves and each other.

This time, the time I'm thinking about, she said she had come to take some photographs. "It's the last time we'll be together and I want to have some photographs." I knew that this was so, that it was over, and great lumps of sadness had crawled into my limbs and lodged there. Val had wandered out of the house and stood waiting to take her place in the small ceremony, the miniature history. We moved around in the untidy yard with its bright red salvia and grey wattle. Val focused and chatted and clicked. I remember this. Clearly.

I have never seen those photographs. Some days after there was a terrible struggle. It was as if we couldn't part without destroying the traces, all the evidence of what had brought us together, made us close. The destruction was beyond our control. It was made out of the kind of hopelessness particular to anger and, looking back, ironic to archaeology. Who considers regret, remorse, those useless feelings — love's waste products? Feelings which make us learn to deal with things, to seal up the past and stare coldly through each other. This changes nothing, and never will. Now we are fixed.

PAMELA BROWN: *Since 1971 Pamela has published ten books of poetry and prose including* New and Selected Poems (Wild and Woolley 1990). *Her next collection,* This World, This Place *is due from UQP in early 1994.*

Pamela lives in Sydney and has travelled several times to Italy and France and also to Vietnam. She has had various occupations and currently works in a library at Sydney University.

Julie McCrossin

Silent Partners

THERE IS a heart shaped tattoo on my upper arm, a scar from a maudlin night of drinking over fourteen years ago. The 'love of my life' had waved me goodbye so I decided to wear my heart on my sleeve. Literally.

The wound has long since healed. Today, my 'lost love' is a dear friend. I even babysit her children and like her man. But one of the great legacies of that early relationship is the friendship I still enjoy with my girlfriend's mother, Cath. She is my ex-mother-in-law you might say.

Initially I loved Cath for her ready acceptance of my relationship with her daughter. Later I realised we would have become good friends whatever way we'd met. We just really like each other.

Every couple of years I travel to the little country town where Cath lives. We gossip for hours about our families and then we move on to politics and 'life'. Cath is nearly seventy and she often tells me stories about growing up in the 40s and married life in the 50s. Last time I saw her she started telling me about her time as a nurse and, in particular, about two women she became friends with during that time.

"I met Barbara an Jane in the early fifties," she told me. "We were working as trainee nurses in the men's surgical ward of a large public hospital in Melbourne and we lived in the nurses' quarters on the hospital grounds. It was pretty grim really. An old, spartan building with high ceilings and inadequate heating. But it was home, if you could call it that, to a hundred or so young women. We were the backbone of the hospital workforce in those days.

"The three of us had rooms on the same floor and we got to know each other pretty well. After the afternoon shifts that often went to midnight, I'd head off to bed exhausted. But Barbara and Jane shared a passion for late night talks. They always said that after the hours of lifting and turning heavy patients, they preferred to unwind and get rid of the nervous energy by talking about their day. The two of them would regularly creep into one of their tiny rooms and I'd hear them whispering into the early hours of those icy Melbourne mornings, while they toasted their feet in front of a single bar radiator.

"You could see their friendship meant a lot to both of them. Especially Jane. She was shy and she hated the enforced intimacy of institutional life. Communal eating and shared bathrooms were an unpleasant shock to her after the privacy of growing up as an only child. 'I'll never get used to the idea that six or seven people have just used the bath before me,' she used to say.

"Barbara was the more confident of the two women. She had a loud voice, strongly held opinions and she really enjoyed telling the rest of us what to do. Her future as a competent but domineering charge nurse was universally predicted from day one.

"That prophecy was ultimately fulfilled," Cath laughed. "Yet in those early days, Barbara revealed yet another side of her personality. At times she could be bombastic, but she had one all important saving grace — a great capacity for loyal friendship. She offered an accepting ear to Jane at a time when Jane desperately needed someone to talk to.

"We were all so young and we'd been thrust into daily contact with sickness and health without being given any opportunity to talk about our feelings. The first year trainees were the lowest rung of a long ladder. We were told how to wash a body and tie up a flopping jaw. 'Nurse, lay out Mr Wilson in 452 please.' But we were never given any tips about how to make sense of Mr Wilson's lonely death or the cruel suffering of his painful illness.

"Sometimes Jane got really upset. Even after her retirement from nursing, she'd still recount an incident which took place just six months into her training.

"She'd been ordered by an impatient nursing sister on a geriatric ward to, 'Go and settle down Mr Cuthbert.' She ran into the room and found a very frail old man crying out, 'No! No!' as a long tube was pushed down his throat to suck the muck out of his lungs. His elderly wife turned to Jane, who was shaking like a leaf, and mumbled bitterly, 'Can't you leave him alone? My mother used to call pneumonia the old man's friend. Now I know why.'

"Nursing made you face this sort of thing all the time and Jane just wasn't up to it. Like so many of us, she'd gleaned a few spiritual certainties from a childhood in suburban Sunday schools. But they crumpled pretty rapidly on the wards.

"I think she started to rely heavily on Barbara's blunt, 'Roll up your sleeves and just do something' approach. Their late night conversations carried Jane through the difficult times in her early years of nursing.

"This all came to an abrupt end just after their final registration exams.

"I wonder if you girls today ever truly realise how strict the 50s were with rules and regulations. Nocturnal visits to other girls' rooms were frowned upon. Barbara and Jane were told, 'This has got to stop.'

"It was Barbara's idea to leave the nurses' home and get a flat together.

They discussed it with me one morning over breakfast in the staff canteen. 'We'll earn more now we're registered. Let's leave them all to it and rent a place of our own.' I remember Jane just laughed and said, 'I'll only have to share my bath with you now!'

"That was the start of a domestic arrangement that was to last for over nearly 40 years.

"Over the years they lost contact with many of the nurses from their training days. Perhaps they felt estranged from their old friends who got married or found better jobs with better pay. They both kept working in major teaching hospitals until they retired.

"But they did maintain close contact with me, even after I married Bill. I remember not long after we were married they came over one day and said they'd decided it made good financial sense to buy a house instead of renting. It never seemed to occur to either of them to do anything other than buy a home together.

"I rang them just after the birth of my first baby and spoke to Jane. I wanted them to come over and see the baby as soon as I got home from hospital. I knew Barbara would love to have the chance to tell me how to wash and feed him properly! She never thought I could get it right when we worked together in maternity.

"They were waiting at my front door the morning I brought the baby home. In fact, over the years Barbara and Jane always loved spending time with our growing brood of children and I welcomed their involvement. Bill was always busy with his medical practice and I was grateful for the chance to discuss the endless questions of child rearing with two loving and practical friends.

"The kids, of course, loved all the special attention from two extra adults. 'You're our two special aunts,' I always said. When I look back, I think we simply swept them both up in the activities of our busy family."

I interrupted Cath to ask a question of my own. "What did you and Bill think about their relationship? Did you ever think it was a little odd? Two women choosing not to marry and never having kids of their own? I mean, they clearly loved children."

"You know, we never spoke about that. In fact, I'd say we openly spoke about Barbara and Jane's relationship on three occasions all those years.

"The first time was when Jane was suddenly taken ill while they were holidaying together one Easter at a fishing village in southern Victoria. Jane woke up in the middle of the night on a Good Friday with a very high temperature. When she tried to walk, she lost her balance. By morning she seemed to be only semiconscious.

"There was only one local doctor in the tiny south coast town where they were staying and she was away on holidays. There wasn't a hospital for miles. In a panic Barbara rang Bill for advice.

"Bill told her to get Jane into a car and bring her straight to his surgery immediately. I heard him say, 'We need to get her into a Melbourne hospital under a specialist we can trust.'

"It was another two hours before the two women arrived. Barbara had to lift Jane out of the back of the car and half carry her up the path. Her face was ashen as she brushed past us with Jane's arm draped around her shoulders. 'She's terribly ill,' she muttered grimly. We helped her make Jane comfortable in the spare bedroom.

"Easter was a bad time to get sick even then. Specialists don't want to take new admissions. It took Bill several hours on the phone to arrange for a bed in a hospital under a physician we all trusted.

"Later I told Bill what had happened during those tense hours while he was on the phone.

"Barbara wouldn't even let me into the room. She insisted she had to do everything for Jane herself. She sat with her the whole time, holding her hand and stroking her hair. She kept touching her and telling her she was going to be all right. She was distraught and almost moaning.

"I never knew till then how much they meant to each other.

"A few years later, they invited us over for lunch at their home. Barbara was very excited about some renovations. 'We want to show you the beautiful job the painters have done. They've been right through the whole house. You'll love it. Bring the kids of course.'

"After the meal, Barbara took us on a tour, chattering about colour schemes and the good price she'd got from the painters. When she took Bill and me into the main bedroom of the house, we noticed they were sharing the same room. Sleeping in bunk beds, one on top of the other.

"Well, nothing was said at the time, but later that night in bed I quizzed Bill, 'Why do you think they sleep in bunks when they could have their own rooms? They've got so much space in that big old house.'"

"And what did Bill think?" I asked.

Cath shrugged, "If Bill did have any theories, he never explored them out loud with me. All he said at the time was, 'I don't know.'

"It would have been about eighteen months after this visit that there was a fundamental change in their domestic arrangements. The first change since they'd moved out of the old nurses' home. Barbara asked a new friend, Pam, another nurse, to move in with them.

"When we went over for lunch a few months later, Barbara had more renovations to show us. 'I've had a marvellous little alcove built for Pam. The builders tried to charge like wounded bulls, but I beat them down,' Barbara crowed.

"Without a trace of self consciousness, Barbara led us back into the bedroom we'd first seen a year or so before. The bunk beds had gone and in their place was a single bed. Jane had now moved into a room of her own at the back of the house. But it was the renovations that Barbara wanted to show off. 'Look. I've built Pam a little closet to sleep in right off my own bedroom. Isn't it cosy? What do you think?' she demanded, gesturing expansively to a small adjoining room through an open archway.

"There was no door. No division at all from her own self proclaimed bedroom," Cath said and then she paused to look at me quizzically.

I leant forward and asked her the question that Cath and her husband had never even asked each other, "Were they lesbians?"

"I don't know," Cath said. "Nobody talked about such things in the circles we mixed in then. But you could cut the air with a knife the whole time Pam was living in that house. Bill and I just kept out of the way. We were all relieved when Pam finally left and got her own place again and we could all get back to normal."

"But do you think they were lesbians?" I insisted.

"I don't really know what to say. But I can tell you that Barbara certainly didn't think so."

"How do you know?"

"Because of something she said to me a few months after Pam left. As soon as Pam was gone, Barbara and Jane went on a cruise together around the Orient. They arranged passage on a small merchant seaman's cargo boat. Only a few passengers. They went to unusual ports. A trip like that was a dream the pair of them had talked about for years.

"Well, they came back rather suddenly. Barbara came to see me as soon as she got home and she was deeply upset. She'd been having a marvellous time she said. Really enjoying getting to know the other passengers. They all ate together at the captain's table and she played the boisterous raconteur. She loved the whole thing. Then one day she overheard one of the women passengers, a retired doctor, refer to her and Jane as 'obvious lesbians'. I'll never forget the look of complete disgust and bewilderment on her face as she said to me, 'Imagine it. Lesbians. They thought Jane and I were *lesbians*.'"

Cath and I just stared at each other for a moment, our eyebrows raised.

After a while, I asked, "Where are they now? Are they still alive?"

"Oh yes. Jane got very ill with cancer for a while. They cut it all out, but it aged her dreadfully. Barbara cared for her at home for as long as she could. But she had her own health problems and it all got too much for her. So about a year ago they sold their home and bought one of those retirement villages. You know, with three stages. Independent units, a hostel and a nursing home. All on the same site. It was a bit of a sacrifice for Barbara because she didn't really need that sort of thing yet. But they wanted to stay together."

"And what about the other woman Pam?"

"Well it's funny you should ask. Barbara was just here to see me a few weeks ago and I asked her about Pam. She told me she'd bought a flat just around the corner from the retirement village and Barbara spends one night a week at her place every week without fail. Barbara goes there *every* Monday night she told me. Jane doesn't like it very much from what I can gather. But she can always use the night buzzer to get nurses to help her if she's in any trouble. So what can she say? Barbara seemed very pleased with herself. She always did like to get her own way."

As I sat staring out the window of my train a few hours later, travelling back home, I went over and over Cath's story in my mind. I kept thinking about Jane in the retirement village on Monday nights. As she sits there alone, does she feel wretched and uneasy? And if she does, could she put into words the reasons for these feelings? Could she explain it even to herself?

Julie McCrossin is 38. University life in the early 70s introduced her to Gay Liberation, the women's movement and all the strategies of political activism. Since that time she has been an outspoken and open advocate of equal rights for gay, lesbian (and now queer) people.

She's been lucky enough to find jobs throughout most of her adult life in which she could promote ideas about social justice. She spent the late 70s and early 80s travelling around Australia with a community theatre group called Pipi Storm in productions about children's legal rights and the impact of computers on the workplace. One show for pre-school children about a little girl called Plain Jane, who grew up on the Sydney Harbour Bridge, led to a short period wearing a red nose.

In 1983, an advertisement in the Sydney Morning Herald swept her into six years as a broadcaster for the ABC, primarily for Radio National on The Coming Out Show and Background Briefing. At the ABC she began moonlighting as a standup comedian with an austere medical character called Dr Mary Hartman. While freelancing in the late 80s, Julie's interest in adult education took her back to Uni and briefly to TAFE as an adult literacy teacher. She now works for a legal tribunal for adults with disabilities called the Guardianship Board, where her interests in journalism and public speaking can be used to promote the rights of vulnerable people. Dr Mary Hartman continues to perform, mainly at conferences as the after dinner speaker.

Julie's story, Silent Partners *is her first piece of fiction.*

LOUISE WAKELING

Golden Anniversary

G ERTRUDE STEIN was right: there is was always will be too much fathering going on. Old progenitor, old bastard. Sylvia gets out of the car. Her father dismounts from the other side, hitches up his surgical truss and walks in like he's Wyatt Earp, a gun riding on each hip.

He was the father she had to have.

Father-dictators. There were just as many around on the international stage these days, not to mention all the faceless fathers, old and young, hanging on in Beijing and Johannesburg and Moscow. But it was the domestic population that had really sky-rocketed, Sylvia thought, climbing the steps of the retirement village. All those petty tyrants wreaking havoc in their own backyards and their own kitchens, the area of their occupation still and always in the minds of those who might have loved them.

Coming out of a sample hostel room, left impeccably neat by a model internee, she and Don pass a clutch of aging sirens at the end of the corridor. Old girls, glasses, fluffy white hair and savage-looking walking sticks, words hanging limp in the air. A general ogling, as father and daughter walk past towards the stairs. The eighty-six year old peacock beside her struts on by, bashfully self-conscious in his almost-best, secretly dirty togs, chest expanding like a life-jacket in the neat waistcoat. In his newly-adopted bachelor role, he has not yet discovered spray-on stain-remover.

He, centre-stage, does not use the bar that runs horizontally along the walls. He walks erect, without looking at the women, but his body slants a little, as though he's executing the high-noon saunter down a dusty main street. He is doing his best to look as though his wife has recently died, rather than merely left him. *(If you don't, I know who will)*.

For a moment, she savours another version: devoted daughter helping dear old Dad choose a place to lay his head. That's his phrase. It is as frosted with Steptoe-overtones as a tequila martini with salt. She is conscious of the tousled white hair, whiter than she remembers it without its customary slick of oil. She feels, in spite of herself, an answering frisson of guilt.

Oh, Daddy

The village guard-dog has no such qualms; down in the narrow garden, he strains at his running leash on the clothes-line, flicking foam from his jaws every time he catches sight of the old man. There is no doubt in his mind, at least, that this one is the enemy.

and there is no doubt about it fathers are depressing

"Let's face it, you and Kevin are levering him out of his home," says Frances. "You can't honestly expect him not to fight back. Wouldn't you?"

Frances is talking about herself, which accounts for the unaccustomed concern for her *de facto* father-in-law. After all, she is the unmentionable shadowy figure in Sylvia's menage, the woman whose unspeakable doings have been immortalised by Don in occasional veiled references to 'what goes on over here'; this coy turn of phrase is usually accompanied by a jerk of the head in the region of upstairs, where Frances is working. That is as close as he cares to approach the idea of his daughter's maverick relationship with another woman.

"So I'm the ogre. The bailiff," Sylvia says. "But it was my mother's home too, you forget that. No-one wants him to win, to sit there triumphant while she ekes out her life in one room. It's not fair."

"For God's sake, eke me no ekes," says Frances. Their relationship has been sorely tried over the past few weeks. It drives her crazy to see Sylvia having to pick up the tab whenever her family whips up a new crisis. "From his point of view it's not fair, either. Why didn't your brother just wait until the old coot died? Let him live in the place, and avoid all this trauma? It'd be a hell of a lot smarter. All he's managed to do is get your father's back up, and lost you your patrimony into the bargain ..."

"Patrimony — huh. By the time all this is over, my patrimony won't be worth a bag of chocolate peanuts."

Chocolate peanuts, or occasionally chocolate sultanas, or even last year's walnuts, were her father's chosen gift when he visited. It was an old habit; when she was a child, Sylvia remembered, he would throw a bag of barley-sugar on the kitchen table on pay-day. He would also do this, by way of a peace-offering, after a particularly vicious fight with Dorothy. These days, Sylvia could tell her own rating from the size and number of the chocolate peanuts he brought. Since the break-up, he'd only given her one opened packet, with four, admittedly large, chocolate brazil nuts in it. The rest, he'd eaten himself.

Back in the hostel room, Sylvia has future-skiied with him down the next slope, the three-stage retirement village, self-care to hostel to nursing-home, planning how much of his home-made '40s furniture he can cram into one room. The one piece he really can't be parted from is the walnut-veneered liquor cabinet that he made himself, with its mirrored interior duplicating wine glasses and bottles of Bailey's Irish Cream. The only problem is that Mumma don't allow no alcohol round here; the rules of this retirement village permit only staff to dispense grog, by way of doctor's orders.

She is weary of explaining the obvious, over and over. Paring down his free-ranging habits to four walls and a Vitalcall button.

Some days he seems frailer than usual, can't seem to get the details of the retirement village donation system straight in his head. Doesn't want to. The CRAGS unit from the local hospital has assessed him as 'frail' but 'alert and able to look after himself'. What really makes him go weak at the knees is the thought of handing over to a retirement village even a portion of his half of the money from the sale of the house. It horrifies him.

Despite the prospect of grasping at more money than he can poke a stick at, Don expects to be looked after at no expense to himself. At the best of times, his attitude to money rivals Volpone's to his gold. The way he reverently handles his bank books often reminds Sylvia of the old Fox. *Open the shrine, that I may see my saint.* Now, with the world breaking apart for him, most of the old certainties gone, money looms larger than ever.

And behind that, it's as though he's waiting for a reprieve, or for Dorothy to suddenly snap back into dutiful wife mode, and pick up where she left off, bentbacked and dazed, shuffling with cups of tea between the house and the cluttered garage where he cloistered himself.

"I can't think any more," he says, in a feeble voice. "I'm depending on you to get me out of this mess. I got so much to organise I don't know whether I'm comin' or goin'."

This from a man who has instructed his solicitor to slap a caveat on the sale of the house, until his 50% of the proceeds could be guaranteed.

"I got a lot to do here," he adds, looking around at the house, the garage, the razed garden. Sylvia's gaze takes in the bare new metal fence, the oleanders and hibiscus bushes of her childhood, grubbed out now or reduced to stumps and armless torsos like war-ravaged statues, the pencil pine in its tub brown and sapless. Her well-meaning brother has achieved overnight what Don had always wanted — the destruction of Dorothy's loved back garden.

Leaning on the side-gate that is bolted and padlocked against intruders, her father is breathless; he winces with pain, real or staged, she can't tell this time. She remembers past drama-queen acts with splinters and fishhooks, but now she doesn't know whether he's being manipulative or not. He never could handle his own pain.

He knows she's trying to dispose of him. She knows he's cunning enough to try to keep more than one jump ahead of her tidy plans. He knows she knows where her mother is. The hostel inspections she chauffeurs him to are the pound of flesh to be exacted, her punishment for helping to throw him out of the house he's lived in for fifty years. Already he's changed his will, cut Dorothy out of his share of her own mother's house, and divided it up amongst the grand-children. So far, their only sins are that they are too wild, or not able to converse with an old man for whom talk is a one-way street. He is already muttering to Sylvia that Kevin has turned the children against him.

"I think they hate me," he says, brokenly, "they only want money from me for vacation camps and for this and that … they never visit me, never even wish me a Happy Birthday, or a Merry Christmas."

Don has the double misfortune to have been born on Christmas Eve.

Sometimes she gets the feeling he's stringing her along. Laughing up his sleeve at the way both adult children are running around like servants of the royal household, with him sitting there like a king-rat in the crumbling palace. And then, there are times when she looks at him, at the soiled shirt and trousers, at the hernia belt bulging from his lower abdomen, and knows that life has finally defeated him.

Perhaps when the house is sold, and he has refused until the 11th hour to bend his mind around the idea of finding somewhere else to live, he will be secretly glad to be thrown out into the street. It is probably another ruse to force her hand, inveigle her to step into her mother's shoes. Even worse, it will be just before Christmas. She can see it now: OLD MAN THROWN INTO STREET BY UNGRATEFUL CHILDREN

Sharper than a serpent's tooth it is to have a thankless child

Sylvia savours the Monty Python image of him in a cardboard box in the middle of West Botany Street. She does not savour the image of him in the spare bed in her son's room. "A fine kettle of fish," he says, bitterly. "It's no good talking about kettles of fish. Where are you going to live — that's what you have to turn your mind to, not why Mum left you …"

"I don't deserve this, I haven't done anything to deserve this … it should never have happened, not at my time of life … your mother should've come back here."

She's used to this one now, should have learned to skirt round it like it's a venomous spider spread-eagled in a web, but like a fascinated insect she can't resist it.

"No, it's not good timing, she should have gone years ago. But she's got the right to put her own life in order, Dad."

Oh for Chrissake let me not get sucked into a long moanin' -low monologue with this one hell of an aggravatin' papa.

"But there was nothing wrong with her life," he yelps back at her, "nothing wrong with our marriage except for these bees she got in her bonnet about this thing and that. I gave her everythink, a world-trip, I built a house on the central coast and then she didn't want to live there, all right, I sold that and we went around the world, I took her everywhere, and she had a wonderful time, until we stayed with her relatives, and then she started to say they were talking about her, and whispering in the next room. She couldn't get along with people, your mother, always thought they were having a go at her ... y'see your mother's been like that ever since I can remember. She's had a go at you, she's said terrible things about you ... "

Oh Daddy look what you're doin', you and your foolin'

These monologues are as unvaried and self-obsessed as the messages on most people's answer-machines.

She talks tough, not wanting to get trapped into shouting at him like she did a few weeks ago, when he finally realised her mother wasn't coming back. Her son went to bed in tears. Frances says Sylvia nearly always raises her voice when she is talking to him on the phone. She doesn't like this at all, especiaily if she is watching *The Bill* in the next room. Sylvia's family is the unwanted baggage in this household; it lies around, destabilising everything and everyone within reach, ticking over like an IRA device, waiting to spew nails. The only difference is that no-one will claim responsibility for the blast.

Sylvia cuddles Frances in the kitchen, lifting a stray wisp of hair to kiss her.

"At least we're still functional," she says. "I think." That doubt hangs above them like the cobwebs festooning the window.

"Don't waste your pity on Dad," Sylvia tells Frances. "When it comes to money, he's as cunning as a shithouse rat."

That clipped, military-style moustache he's affected for the past few years twitches. He likes being appreciated by the fluffy-haired brigade. He's warming to the possibility of a good old mag with some of the old-timers who kicked around the area in his youth. A bit of a lair, her mother always called him. In 1933 he used to wear turned-up collars, Brylcreemed hair parting like the Red Sea down the middle, a full-length leather jacket. At one stage he rode a Harley. To a 16 year-old Minnehaha-plaited girl with pom-poms on her slippers, he must have seemed exciting.

Sylvia looks at him sideways; in his twenties, she has seen from old photos, he was a medium-sized man. But these days he seems to be shrinking more and more. The amazing vanishing man. This doesn't prevent him from hoisting his hernia chestwards for the march-past in front of the old girls.

Back there, the sirens are still following him with their eyes. They have completely lost interest in talking to each other, and are watching her father out of sight. There aren't many single men in the village. At this age the fathers are becoming a rarity: a sighting of one is as thrilling as a fleeting glimpse of a Tasmanian tiger. It's a hopeful sign that at least here he'll be in demand.

The manageress tells Sylvia, "We like to try and keep a balance of men and women here, so you might find we can jump him up the list more quickly, him being a gentleman and all."

Don is a veteran of a 50 year old marriage that was more like trench warfare, but the old girls don't know that. He also has a double hernia, a leaking heart-valve and a prostate disorder that makes him want to piss every ten minutes, and will probably result soon in a burst bladder. But they don't know that either.

"You know what," he says, "the women in this retirement village are terrible old. Oh, they're very frail, some of 'em."

Descending the stairs, the manageress bobs below her like an overripe eggplant she saw once on the Grand Canal, buoyant in the wake of another boat. Sylvia wonders if she, too, is marvelling at how many 86 year old domestic tyrants are unlucky enough to be left by their wives in the same year they might have (but didn't) celebrate their golden anniversary.

Dorothy couldn't have done it a messier way, staging her 19th nervous breakdown against a lurid background of lithium hallucinations and paranoid fantasies. In her right mind, she could not bring herself to leave him; she couldn't let go the idea of the house, her mother's house. She could only go like this, taken raving, reeling in and out of clarity. Giving over to others all sense of responsibility.

"It's a house of misery," she says. "I never want to go back."

In the space of a week Dorothy jumped from the walnut veneered marital bed to a narrow high pallet in the psychiatric ward of the local hospital, and from there to a broom-cupboard. A warm and cosy one, in a hostel for the financially down-and-out, but still a broom-cupboard. The hostel, actually only 15 minutes due south from her old home, is directly opposite a technical college and overlooks a busy side-street in a suburban shopping centre. To her, it feels like a different part of the country. It's as though she inhabits an alien time-zone. As though the time with him, 50 years of on-off misery, has come to an abrupt end. Like time on the college clock she can see from her window, handless and giving nothing away.

Her leaving him in this manner was tasteless. As for timing, it could only be described as appalling, a few months before Christmas, a few months after the uncelebrated 50 year anniversary. And right smack in the middle of a recession, with real-estate prices spiralling lower than ever. Hadn't Sylvia been telling her to leave him ever since she could say the word 'divorce'? Her mother might not even have done it at all if Kevin hadn't stepped in and orchestrated the separation.

She had loved Don, in a funny kind of way, but years of his persecution and rages had leached whatever was left of that emotion. For anyone. The residue, she siphoned off to Kevin, the desired, protective male she'd always longed for, Kevin, who is alone again after a brief, doomed fling with Helen, the woman he's been sharing rented accommodation with since he left his second wife. Still, "I love every hair on that man's head," Dorothy said of Don, only a few years back. Which only goes to show how tasteless she could be.

"Y'mother wouldn't listen to me," he shouts. "How was I to know she was takin' too many of them pills?"

The best of all possible spouses in the best of all possible worlds. "The great I-Am," her mother calls him. One of the biggest hurdles he's had to face, apart from the loneliness of racketing around in an almost empty house and, even worse, having to get his own meals, is the embarrassment. The very first thing he said when Ita, the hospital social worker, told him Dorothy had decided to leave him was, "What am I going to tell the neighbours?"

"She's bonkers," he says, to Sylvia. "She's been bonkers ever since I first knew her. The way she used to fight with all the people she knew, and complain that this one and that one was criticising her behind her back, and talking about her in the shop ... "

"Well, if she's bonkers you ought to feel well shot of her," she says, with cold logic. If she hears all this one more time she'll go bonkers herself.

"Tell Sylvia not to turn her back on him in that house," Dorothy tells Kevin. "He's a very violent man."

Nick and Rita are a Yugoslav couple who speak very little English. They don't know what goes on in her parents' home; to them, Don and Dorothy are a sweet old couple. Over the years they've invited them to weddings and Christmases and plied them with home-made sour wine from the grape-vine that lies supine on their backyard trellis, and never once imagined the two of them were anything but Darby and Joan. When they hear about the break-up, they are worried about Dorothy. They feel sorry for Don. They are also worried who their new neighbours will be when the house is sold, as Sylvia tells them it must be. Maybe they will be Muslim.

Her mother wanders into Nick and Rita's, a few days before the shadows in the front room finally infiltrate the venetian blinds. She shakes hands with both of them, laughing.

"I just want you to know that I'm alright now, I've been unwell but I'm better now. Don't worry about me, I'll be fine."

Her mother is lying in bed in her front room, eating a boiled egg and bread and butter oh-so-slowly on the tray Sylvia has brought. It is the tray she uses for her son when he is sick in bed. He is not happy that she's taken it. He wants it back. He does not love his grandmother or his grandfather because he perceives, with the unfailing insight of a child, that they are not really interested in him. Before grandmother left, grandad was a potential source of chocolate peanuts and forbidden lollies, sometimes slipped to him behind Sylvia's back. He, too, has noticed that the gifts have abruptly stopped. No more packets of no-name no-interest sweets that Sylvia spirits away to the back of a top cupboard.

"When is all this ever going to end?" he asks Frances, after yet another long visit to grandad's.

"You're a good girl," her mother tells Sylvia. Sylvia feels guilty. There are times when she doesn't like her mother very much, when she remembers how one-sided their relationship has been for many years. Her mother sees things in black and white: if Sylvia spends time alone with her father, then she too is the enemy, a traitor. I'm not a good girl, she thinks. And you're a selfish, paranoid, unloving so-and-so who hasn't lifted a finger to help me out when I needed it and now you expect me to mother you. You never even pick up the phone to ring me up. You've probably forgotten the number, or you don't want to have to make small talk with Frances. Basically, at some stage along the line, you simply wiped me. One part of your brain pays lip-service to maternal emotions — and the other part? Parts?

She helps her mother put on the nightgown she was given by the Salvos for doing voluntary work, noticing that she has no underwear on. In fact, she doesn't seem to own any underwear at all any more. All the clothes she wears now came from the Salvos. Sylvia has never seen her mother in the apricot skirt and blouse she bought her the Christmas Dorothy had her last breakdown, although she has asked her about them several times.

Lately, hurt piled on hurt, her mother has started to give her back some of her early presents. Not the antiques, just the salt-shakers and the things she doesn't want any more, like the book that she and Frances wrote together and that she's sure her mother has never read.

"I never laid a finger on your mother," her father shouts at her, over the phone.

"Oh, yeah?" Sylvia shouts back. "I suppose she pulled her own hair out and threw herself on the floor, and gave herself those huge bruises on her forehead and under her chin. I suppose she did all that herself, did she?"

"That's crap. You're making it all up."

"Oh, yes, my memories are crap." She has a brief flash of him raging at her mother over something, flinging himself about at the wheel of the Vanguard. Then, the next instant, he was driving straight at the cliff-edge on the old Central Coast highway, hurtling towards the white barrier. She has never forgotten her own elongated scream harpooning out from the back seat, the only thing that made him swerve. Even now, the memory has the power to jolt her awake in dreams of falling away into empty air.

"You're both lying. Your mother always bruised easily. She was always falling on the floor. You all blame me for everythink that's happened around here, but listen, your mother's been going off like this ever since we was first married and living in the shop. She started worrying that women were talking about her, so I took her to the doctor's and he told me to take her away for a holiday, she was working too hard, and I said to him 'Where am I going to get the petrol for that?' There was a war on and you couldn't get much petrol in those days. But he gave me a couple of coupons and I took her away for a holiday and she was fine after that, laughing and happy, singing to herself in the salon ... "

When Sylvia walks into the room in Pacific House her mother is lying asleep in the bed, her mouth hanging ajar. She looks small and frail in the new nightgown Sylvia bought for her. Through the window Sylvia can see the blue waters of the Bay, and feel the salt breeze, which is like her childhood. Wet and lost costumes, the tight and crusty feeling of sunburnt skin, the bitter after-taste of her parents' arguments. The even bitterer taste of the sleeping tablets her mother gave her to calm Sylvia's hysterical weeping after their own deadly battles.

She puts some more underwear in the cupboard beside the bed, tumbles some fruit into a bowl, and goes out to talk to the nurse. At the door she turns, and her mother stirs. Her eyes flicker open. She looks straight at Sylvia. Those eyes are liquid, dilated and dark, like a snake's eyes, without depth, but there is something there — hostility? fear? recognition? Sylvia can't tell. Her mother closes her eyes again, turns her head away.

Don is sitting in Sylvia and Frances' dining-room on Boxing Day. Frances is upstairs. He has just finished eating his lunch, having casually thrown into the conversation that the 'chick' who bought his bedroom furniture was all bum and legs, and the sliced turkey breast doesn't look like turkey; it's not dark enough, and the calamari salad is tougher than the deep-fried ones he's eaten down at the boat-club. He's still a member there, even though he's been boatless for years.

"Look at this lump on my chest — I've squeezed it and something black came out but I've still got this lump here."

Sylvia looks at the lump among the tendrils of white hair and thinks twice about finishing her own lunch.

"It's a fine kettle of fish I'm in," he says, next time she rings. "I didn't ask for all this in my old age. It comes at a terrible time, I'm not a well man, I'm getting terrible thin, I've got a weak heart and I can't go into hospital until all this is over."

Then, it's as though he's reading from a totally different score.

"Strickland and Olive have taken up with each other—he's going to take her to a sheep-station and then to Tahiti except that this week some volcano or other has erupted in Tahiti and lava is flowing all over the place so they can't go there now … "

Lava come back to me, for Chrissake. Sylvia holds the phone half a metre away and duck-noises come out of the mouthpiece as he bores on and on and on about his seventy-six year old sister Olive who has changed her name to Julie and taken up with an old flame. A minute or two later, he is telling her all over again how his sister has met up with his old mate Strickland, and is planning to be out of town soon (around about when Don is due to take up residence in the box in the road). For some reason he doesn't twig to the fact that she'd do anything to avoid having him stay in her apartment. Even when she's not planning to be out of town whooping it up, she has mysterious headaches that she has to see her doctor about, and which somehow prevent her offering Don her spare bedroom. Instead of being upset about this, he throws himself excitedly into the fairy-story of Olive-Julie and Strickland, tells Sylvia a hundred times about how he was responsible for getting them together again after all these years and how much money Strickland's got and how he knows a lot of people and he's a big man.

"Is all this going to do something for you, Dad? Is he going to find you somewhere to live?"

He is not listening. Her father had wanted to be a big man, too, but somehow he just shrank, things shrivelled up on him, riches slipped through his fingers.

Maybe that's why, now, he's started to carry wads of money around with him in his wallet. He's hidden a strongbox somewhere, maybe at his sister's unit, or under the garage floor. *Good morning to the day; and next, my gold!*

Sylvia asks him about the rolls of money Kevin saw him fumbling with one day in the street. She imagines him mugged in the shopping-centre, or lying in his own blood on the garage floor.

"Don't you worry about it," he says waspishly.

To Don, Strickland is 'moneybags' now. He tells Sylvia that Strickland and Olive are not going to get married. Olive-Julie is 76 and Strickland is 80, and she's buried three husbands already. His wife died two years ago, and it seemed like a good time to look Olive up. He'd fancied her all those years ago although she said she didn't want to meet him again because he was always a bit of a fop, but now he had time on his hands and a bundle of money and he just wanted to have a good time ...

"It's a quarter to eleven, Dad."

"Is that the time? I thought it was ten o'clock."

"It was when you rang me over three-quarters of an hour ago."

"Yes, well," he says, revving up again, "I passed the driving test with flying colours. I don't have to sit for another one for twelve months. . ."

He says this with relish because he knows she wanted him to fail.

Her voice reveals neither surprise nor disappointment. Her father behind the wheel of his manual is as good as a hired assassin. A hard-driving papa, even without the hat old men seem inevitably to wear. Anyone foolish enough to ride with him totters shell-shocked from the car. Most of them prefer to walk any number of kilometres home, however dark and stormy a night it is, rather than spend five minutes in the front seat watching him dangle and grind between first and second gear in the face of an oncoming car.

"Yes, well, think about where you're going to live," she urges him, trying to head him off at the pass.

"I'll just have to take my bags and sleep in the park," he says, morosely.

Oh, Daddy

"For God's sake, Dad, you've never had to sleep rough in your life," Sylvia says.

"Yes I have, I slept in a tent when we was workin' out at Warragamba pipeline."

"Dad, that was hardly sleeping rough. You were young, and sleeping out was an adventure. Don't talk nonsense. Of course no-one expects you to sleep in the park."

For a fleeting moment, she takes a strange comfort in the thought that, with a bank-roll as fat as Ma Rainey's, and big enough to choke on, he wouldn't last long on a park-bench.

there's no doubt about it fathers are depressing
Oh, Daddy

112

LOUISE WAKELING: *Outside on the balcony, my green chimes sound in the small-est breeze. When they knock together gently in the pre-dawn, I wake up thinking of temple bells.*

Domesticity. Chaos. Attempts at order. The setting is Outer Suburban Un-fashionable, but there are trees, thousands of them, outside my window, and rainbow lorikeets squabbling and whistling in the umbrella tree. And beyond them, yes, blinkered neighbours clinging hard to suburban conformity. Most times, there is silence and solitude. I like writing here. Not a cappuccino machine in sight, but I can see the foothills of the Blue Mountains from the balcony, can imagine Pemulwy and the last remnants of the Parramatta tribe fighting pitched battles with the white invaders.

Wide, dusty red roads lie under these house-infested hills, and under them, in unyielding clay, the footprints, middens and carvings of the lost tribes. In the local quarry, now a park, the exposed rock strata are 25,000 years old. When you write about the past, as I am doing in a historical narrative set in Western Syd-ney, it is not surprising that sometimes this distant landscape becomes more real, more tangible, than the present. Occasionally, apropos of some oblique comment, I have startled colleagues by announcing a list of items found in the belly of a large grey-nurse shark caught at Balmain in 1884, or the sleeping-out habits of the Harris Park larrikins and their molls. I think they'd rather me write a novel about a P & C bargain bus crawl around the factory outlets of Surry Hills.

Louise Wakeling is currently Community Writer-in-Residence with the Fair-field/Liverpool Disabled Person Resource centre in Western Sydney, where she conducts writing workshops for people coping with mental illness. Her poetry, short stories, reviews and articles have been published in numerous anthologies, as well as in journals such as: Westerly, Mattoid, Going Down Swinging, Southerly, Outrider, Aspect, Poetry Australia, Australian Literary Studies *and* BURN.

She has co-edited and co-authored several books, including a biography of Ada Cambridge, Rattling Orthodoxies *(Penguin 1991), and a collection of les-bian autobiographies,* Words from the Same Heart *(Hale & Iremonger 1988). Her first novel,* Saturn Return, *was published by Hale & Iremonger in 1990. She is working on her second novel, a historical/utopian narrative, as part of a Ph.D. in Creative Writing at the University of NSW.*

She nearly always bites off more than she can chew.

HELEN PAUSACKER

Masturbation Fantasy Gone Wrong

I AM sitting at my typewriter. I am working back late at the office. I think there's no-one else here. But then I sense someone's presence in the room. It must be the cleaners. They usually come in at a quarter to six. I look at my watch. It's half past five. They must be early.

The room is carpeted and I don't hear footsteps ... I just feel hands — a woman's hands. She's undoing my bun, pulling the pins out, taking out the combs.

"You've got beautiful hair," she says. "Why don't you wear it out more often? I just want to stroke it. It's so soft."

I lean back, letting my body rest against hers, feeling her warm, round breasts against my back. I look up at her, over my shoulder.

"I thought you'd gone home," I say. "Are you working back, too?"

"Not now, I'm playing now."

She has her hands on my breasts, and my nipples are erect, my whole body is stiffened with excitement.

"We've only got ten minutes before the cleaners come," she says. "Why not come into my office, where we can at least lock the door."

She is one of the engineers and has her own office. I work in the library as a library assistant and anyone can walk in any time.

She picks me up in her arms. She's a strong woman, and she's covering my face with kisses as she carries me in and sits me on her desk. My desk's all messy and covered with in-trays full of half-done work and half-processed books. Hers has nothing on it, and the office is neat and tidy ... like everything else about her. She works back a lot.

She unbuttons my blouse and takes it off, then cups her hands round my breasts, and leaning down, takes the nipple into her mouth. She bites it and I gasp, half with pleasure, and half with pain. She smiles.

"Just keeping you on your toes," she remarks.

My toes are tingling, the whole of my body is tingling. She holds one of my nipples between the thumb and forefinger of one hand; while the other hand plays with the inside of my leg, starting at the knee and working upwards inside my skirt. Her hand glides over my pantyhose. My cunt is moist with anticipation. I could almost come now.

Then we hear a noise.

"It's the cleaners," she says. "Quick, put your clothes on. They mustn't know."

"I never knew you were gay till today."

"I'm not," she snaps. "Will you come back to my place? I'll pay for your time."

"Why pay me? I want it too."

"Time is money. I enjoy my work, and I get paid for it. I pay the cleaning woman for cleaning my house, and I want to pay you."

Oh god, what have I landed myself with here? I'm trying to stop myself thinking about Trudi. We've been broken up for three months now. I got her letter today, saying that she definitely didn't want to get back together again. I haven't even masturbated for three months now. I just lost interest. I always used to fantasise about her when we were on together, and I was having a play on my own. I'm trying to break the habit. I thought it would be safe to dream up a nameless business woman. But I've landed myself with a closet case, who wants to pay me.

The money business ... Well, you know where that comes from, Helen. You've only had two days' work this week and you've spent all your waking hours telling yourself that you're not worried. Of course, when you relax, the worries will come to the surface. Perhaps you'd better spend more time in the day looking for work.

But back to the business woman. What am I going to do? I don't want to do it for money.

But she doesn't want the sex without the money. Perhaps you'll have to compromise. What about giving the money away? That would keep you both happy.

I am at Simon's house, and explaining my problem to him. Simon is the Gay Conference treasurer and I'm on the collective.

"I just wondered, Simon, you see ... there's this business woman who wants to pay me for sex. I feel funny accepting the payment, and I know the conference is short of money so I thought I could perhaps donate it to the conference fund, given we're so short of money. I don't want to say no, but I've got a guilty conscience. I expect I should work on her gay identity instead, and make her feel happy about being gay, so that she doesn't need to pay me off. But she's got money and the gay movement needs money ..."

"Why are you so jumpy?" asks Simon. "What's wrong with prostitution? It's just work, and you're short of work yourself. We don't need guilt money."

"But I'd enjoy the sex with her," I protest.

"Hmm," says Simon, and he grins quizzically at me. "And you can't enjoy work? You seem a bit mixed up. Have a think about it. Keep the money if you like, or give it to the conference collective. It doesn't worry me. We'll raise the money for the conference somehow, either way."

Perhaps I feel upset that I'm being bought off. That I feel it's contradictory to work in the gay movement and yet to creep around in the office with this engineer, hiding it all. Bloody business woman. Bloody gay politics. I want Trudi.

Your cunt's drying up. Keep masturbating. You've got to start getting interested in other women sometime. Start now, in your fantasy. Let's face it. It's your own mind that created the situation. You created your own story and put your own obstacles in it, and now you can just get rid of them. Just go to her flat and do it. Forget the money. Wipe that episode from the story. Get on with it.

I am at her flat now, and she's taking my clothes off. This time she's started with my pantyhose, drawing them off slowly and running her hands up my legs. She unbuttons my blouse and slips her hand in, feeling my breasts.

Her hands are like sandpaper. My cunt is as dry as a bone. The sofa I'm sitting on is hard and cold. I hate her.

"Keep your bloody money," I shout. "I'm going home."

I slam the flat door and run out barefoot into the night crying. My blouse is flapping open.

I do up my pyjama top. Trudi, Trudi, I don't want to forget you. And your letter's lying on the floor beside my bed. I don't want a nameless business woman. I want you to write and say you've changed your mind. I want to ring you up and say hello, and hear your voice. But it's three in the morning.

Try again tomorrow night. You'll get the knack eventually. It takes time ... Go to sleep.

HELEN PAUSACKER: *I have been writing stories and poems since I was about seven, both for my own enjoyment and for my sister and friends to read. Six years older than me, my sister also told me stories and sat on the end of my bed, while we together composed my bedtime stories. She decided to become a professional writer and subconsciously I felt I needed to seek a different niche, so I kept my writing as a hobby. I have continued to fill my bottom drawer with stories and poems.*

Seeking new fields, I studied Javanese wayang (shadow puppetry) at the age of twenty, a training which I thoroughly enjoyed, but which I realised I could never gain proficiency in, nor earn a living from. I still play in a Javanese

116

gamelan orchestra and am currently translating a wayang script into English.

On my return from Java, I learned to type and have held a large number and variety of part time and administrative and library jobs over the years. I have never learned to drive nor seen the need for a washing machine, television or record player. I am a bit of a Luddite. The careerist, up-market business woman represents the 'other' — the unknown and the fascinatingly incomprehensible.

I have been a lesbian for over 20 years and involved in lesbian and gay male 'coalition' activism and publications since 1979.

A Fine Day for an Outing

"**I**S THAT the paper boy?" Dora twitched back the curtains, looking at the bald new day. Outside the morning glowed with the freshness of Spring and down on the Harbour it was just possible to make out the green and gold ferry steaming around towards the jetty.

"No, Betsy would have barked." Anne leaned over and poured a cup of percolated coffee, then patted the table. "Come and have some breakfast."

But she could see immediately that even the homey fragrance of coffee was not going to entice Dora this morning. Dora sat down heavily at the table opposite her, still absorbed in thought, and took a jerky sip of coffee. For a brief moment Anne could have sworn her hand trembled slightly.

"Such a terrible business," Dora said, "They've no right!"

"It will all blow over soon." Anne stirred a lump of sugar into her coffee. "These things are seven day wonders. P'raps it won't be so bad ... might even be a relief."

"Not so bad? It's all right for you I suppose." There was an edge to Dora's voice. "You don't stand to lose as much — an academic, and in archaeology. It's not the same."

Anne sipped her coffee in silence. Really, Dora was going too far. She looked at her companion critically. Dora's graduation photo on the piano showed a young woman with lustrous hair and frank hazel eyes. Now her hair was thinning and her eyes were like a warning.

Anne snapped a water biscuit and nibbled at a morsel. "You've retired, darling, and your super's assured. You're exaggerating a little."

"Superannuation has nothing to do with it. In our day, certain things were kept private. We didn't rush around shouting our most intimate secrets from the tree-tops. And the newspapers respected one's privacy too. It was a discreet age," Dora insisted, "and all the better for it. Now it's all Mardi Gras and picketing Parliament. And so-called gays running around trumpeting Jason this and Jodie that ... Really, these young ones would take it on themselves to expose Leonardo!"

There was silence for a moment. Anne realised the effort was up to her.

"Perhaps the press will leave it alone," she said soothingly. "After all, where's the public interest in how people live their lives — even prominent ones?"

"The press? Good heavens, the press will have a field day. The *Telegraph Mirror* will run a scurrilous story, complete with name, rank and serial number and the *Herald* will quote it in toto in its editorial and comment gravely on the *Telegraph Mirror's* lapse in taste."

Dora spread a thin film of marmalade on her toast. "Nothing new there, of course," she conceded. "Did I ever mention Liberace v The Daily Mail? The *Mail's* music critic described him — and I quote — 'A sniggering, snuggling, chromium-plated, scent-impregnated, luminous, quivering, giggling, fruit-flavoured, mincing ice-covered heap of mother love!' But then ... the *Daily Mail* has such a way with adjectives. They topped it off by calling him 'everything that He She or It can ever want'. Well, naturally, Liberace sued for defamation, swearing he never was, never had been, and never would be any of the above." She nibbled at an orange segment. "He made a squillion out of it, of course. And so he should — such an invasion of privacy. You can always rely on the law to get it right — even if for all the wrong reasons."

"The law's such a minefield. Trust you to take up such a difficult area," Anne said, her voice like balm.

"Oh, difficult, my foot. The law's quite simple. It's people who are difficult."

"But it wasn't easy for you, being a woman judge in those days. You were such a trail blazer."

"The *only* woman judge. It's true. You had to be better than the men, back then. I know — because I was."

"Remember the Chief Justice when you were nominated for the bench? And the day you were sworn in. He looked like an apoplectic fish! And he insisted on calling you Mr Justice Simmonds. Remember?"

"As if I'd ever forget! The howls of laughter reached all the way to Granny's Column."

"So you suggested ... that's right, a compromise — all the judges called plain Justice — men, too."

"Yes, William accepted the situation eventually, of course — and me too." Dora permitted herself a smile. "He had to accept it. No judgment of mine was ever overturned on Appeal. Not one." Even now there was an edge of triumph that retirement and the long stretch of ordered days could not erase. "Towards the end, William read all my judgments first and simply concurred with everything I said. Poor man, he was such a Whig! Well, somebody had to drag him screaming into the 20th century."

She sat for a moment ruminating and ran her fingers through her hair. "I might go to the hairdressers today."

"Today? Whatever for? You had it done on Monday."

119

"Well, it's such a fine day — we could drive up to the Mountains. Stay overnight at Leura. We'll avoid all the publicity that way."

"Leura! A lovely idea ... the fresh air and the bush. It always takes me back ... reminds me of our time in the Land Army."

"Absolutely," said Dora, leaning forward, preparing to take over the reminiscence. "We were swimming down in Hunter's Lake ... practically deserted ... only a couple of other women there ... it was twilight I seem to recall."

"But the sun ... " Anne cut in.

"Yes, yes ... I'm coming to that. The sun was just setting behind the trees and the water was ablaze with orange light. It was perfect."

"Perfect," Anne echoed, "and then suddenly you took me in your arms — and kissed me! Just like that!"

"And we looked up, guilty as sin and there were Jean and Norah..."

" ... kissing each other! Laugh! My god, how we all laughed." Anne chuckled "But I was terrified — you were so brave."

"Tssk, that was nothing. I always feel the real risk I took was with Jack. I came so close to marrying him, you know. It was expected."

Anne rose to the occasion. "Jack? Marry Jack? Of all people! What happened? Why didn't you?"

"But don't you see? I met you and it was no use then. Pretending, I mean." She settled back in the chair. "Not that we ever did much pretending, now I think of it." She ran her hand over her papery cheeks. "Oh, we'd go to the theatre and he'd buy me chocolates and then he'd drive me home. My parents thought it was a perfect match. So many marriages must have been based on total innocence ... because we would have, you know ... marry, I mean."

In the distance, farther up the hill, they heard the newsboy's whistle, one long shrill, then a short chirrup, like an echo. Dora sat perfectly still.

Anne covered the moment of tension. "So what happened?"

"It began to dawn on me, how much more I enjoyed being with you ... how I looked forward to our evenings together at the pictures ... or the golf course ... or just talking ... and I realised I was postponing evenings with Jack so I could be with you ... and the penny dropped."

"What on earth did you tell Jack?"

"The truth. I said there wasn't much point in our keeping company any more. I wasn't going to marry him, or anyone else for that matter. I'd just have to risk staying single But Jack sat there. I must've told you this ... we were in Prince's eating Sydney rock oysters ... I always remember that ... I can still see Jack, even now, sitting there ... fork poised over a huge oyster shell. And a single tear trickling down his face. He looked so white and shocked. It was a truly awful moment," she gave a stifled giggle. "But the dreadful thing was, with poor Jack so upset — crying — all I could think of was the Walrus and the Carpenter ... " Dora sighed. "Everyone said we were a perfect couple ... and as events were to prove, so we were in a ... "

Dora was interrupted by the shrill blast of the newsboy outside. Betsy growled for a moment and then began yapping. Dora heaved herself up from the table and began fumbling in her purse. She opened the front door and Anne could hear the squeal of the paper boy's cart coming to a stand-still and the jingle of coins as he scrabbled for change. She heard Dora's muffled voice, "We'll be taking the *Telegraph* as well today."

Dora returned with the papers and spread the *Herald* on the breakfast table, swiftly turning the pages, scanning them for the article.

"It's rather like the Queen's Honours," she said with a laugh, adjusting her reading glasses.

Anne relaxed a little, vulgarity was heartening in the circumstances.

"There's the usual list of actors." Dora muttered. "And Joan, well that's no surprise, she's never had to hide anything — so easy in the theatre."

She bent over the papers absorbed in her search. For an instant Anne had a poignant memory of all those years ago when Dora would look up examination results, her eyes flashing with confidence and delight. But now she took off her reading glasses and laid them flat on the table.

"What is it?" Anne asked sharply.

"So strange," Dora's voice was uneven. "Only two judges mentioned by name — and both men. Jack, of course, and Harold ... But no one else."

"That — that's wonderful," Anne said carefully. "Such a relief."

Dora gave a slow nod. "A tremendous relief," she said.

She stood up and went over to the window. Very deliberately, she drew back the lace curtain, looped the cord around it and hooked it back by the window. Sunlight streamed in, lighting up her mahogany desk. Outside on the Harbour the ferry ploughed its steady, ritual course.

"It's a fine day," said Dora and her tone was suddenly firm and jubilant. "Such a fine day ... and these young ones ... these radical groups ... they can't even get their research right. It's so shoddy! That's what concerns me. There's nothing for it," she said, picking up her fountain pen, "It's up to me. Someone has to set the record straight."

ROBERTA SNOW *is in love with the mystery of the mask. On her walls are masks she found in New Orleans and Prince Edward Island. Wearing a mask is like skating over the sea or floating in a hot air balloon and landing on another continent; it means you can dance longer, laugh louder and write faster. It means freedom and escape.*

ALISON LYSSA

The Meeting

THERE'S A large hall. There are a lot of people not taking any notice of me. I can't work out whether that's good, or worse.

I'd munch my way through the wine glass, only it's not disposable.

I wasn't here when the credentials were given out. I don't mean the name tags, the agenda, the wine, the pastries filled with squashed fish, I mean the coping credentials. The ones everyone else has got and I haven't.

You'd think in a crowd this size there'd be someone for me. I try one or two and get the grasshopper treatment. That's when you think they're concentrating but as soon as they see a more likely stalk their eyebrows twitch. They're going to jump straight over you.

If my mother came in now I'd yell at her. Wouldn't do any good. Now that he's dead she said she doesn't have to worry about anything.

There's a hush. As if I've spoken out loud, and everybody's listening. They're not. I reach around the back of the waiter, seize a glass and say everything. Words spilling out.

Tell me, tell me what I have to do to stop my mother being mean. She won't buy herself a heater, she won't let me get rid of the mice, she won't let me throw out the leftovers, stinking since last time. I wrap them in newspaper, pile them on the landing. While I'm in the bathroom peeing with my head in my hands, I hear her unwrapping. She's discovered my stealings. She wants her left-overs back. Her decaying chops, her rotten dishrag.

We fight. Pulling newspaper and stinking chicken between us.

Why? I shout. Why is my mother mean to my mother? And he left her enough money, the bastard.

Nobody can hear me. They're passing out the door. I want to follow, but they've left half eaten trays of battered mushrooms. I wanted them to carry me out of here on their shoulders. Let them go without me. I'll eat the plates clean.

I didn't want to be here by myself. I should apologise.

Sorry. As if sorry could bring about reconciliation.

It doesn't.

Sorry I hurt you. Sorry I tried to drive you away without driving you away. Sorry I tried to change you so I wouldn't have to drive you away.

Sorry I tried to change myself so I wouldn't have to drive you away.

Sorry none of that worked and we were both so angry one of us had to say, It's over.

Sorry it was me. You wouldn't come back now if I was wearing hair shirts of sorries.

My mother wouldn't have thrown away a perfectly good lover. She had enough sense not to push anyone so far they'd fall out of reach of sorry.

But they got away all the same. My sister married a Sheik and emigrated. My father had gout and died.

You and I will die without one another.

My father was always saying sorry. Sorry to be complaining, the lid is off the tomato sauce bottle.

I'm sorry, said my mother.

No, I'm sorry, said my father.

Well, I'm sorry, said my mother.

No, I'm sorry, said my father.

I wonder if she left the lid off so he'd notice how busy she was keeping everything. She used to wash the empty tomato sauce bottles and stack them in the cupboard where dad could make them fall out when he went looking for matches. He stood in the tidal wave of bottles trying to be a gentleman. Gentlemen are never angry with their wives.

You won't get away with it this time, dad. I'm coming back to make you angry. Grab the bottle dad. Throw it. The room is so full you've got to throw it. Throw it.

Blood streams down the wall. Now my mother knows what to do. She takes the box of envelopes her husband brought home and stuffs them in the washing up water shrieking, I will not address another envelope.

He stands on the kitchen table kicking butter from his shoe. She passes him the whip, while my sister hides in the broom cupboard pretending to be a horse. Mother lies on the edge of the table, her back striped with red. Father shakes the salt gently like a blessing.

I'm sorry.

Scream, mother. Throw him and his envelopes out of the house. I have come back to make you scream. If you got away from him you could do something you wanted. I wouldn't let you be lonely, mother.

She's not listening to me. Mother, Don't you trust me? I know I was on his side then. He and I used to think you were stupid, but I've changed. Be angry with him, please.

She won't. She's listening to him. He's telling us all about the virtues of envelopes. He's going to give us words to put in those envelopes; we're going to stick on the stamps and take them to the post-office. People are going to read his precious words and be moved.

The kitchen filled with thunder against the things that were wrong — gambling, prostitution, drunkenness had eroded his fellow man, now communism was wearing away at the heart. The time had come for honest citizens to bring the world back to goodness, my father was going to tell them how. And we couldn't even put the lid back on the tomato sauce bottle.

My father jammed the lid on as if he was loading a battleship. Dark sauce from the rim squelched onto his fingers.

Don't be cross.

A roar rushed from his heart to his lips, but his lips were wedged shut.

The disappointed roar sank into his bell sucking after it an awful hunger. Lamingtons, milkshakes, marmalade, nothing was ever enough. We were never enough.

Well, I'm sorry. My mother plunged the washing up into the sink, felt the arthritis coming on, and was clumsy.

I'm sorry, look what you've done, he cried, bending down to cut his finger on the broken bowl.

He's going to be helpful, he's going to fill the kitchen with the sweeping of the pieces. He's going to find the tin-opener under the table. What is that doing there? Can't you ever put anything in the proper place? He's going to want the dustpan and hand broom and my mother won't know where to find them. He's going to find my sister's *Superman* Comic.

I've got to get him out of here. Let my sister whinny out the backdoor with Superman stuffed up her bloomers, I will go in with my father and write envelopes faster than anyone. I will not waste an envelope. If I make a mistake I'll hide it in my blazer pocket and throw it out at school.

Good girl, said my father, you've got brains.

And you? If I had been different, would you still be my lover?

There's people coming in, I think everyone's breaking now for coffee. Will they notice I stayed out here? I want somebody to notice, make their way over here bearing two cups of coffee, and discover that I might look eccentric, but I know how to make a person feel witty and wanted. It's a skill, learned at my father's knee. I can also polish shoes, find lost car keys, press a dinner suit and address a mean envelope. And when I'm in the mood I can look pretty good in a dinner suit.

Make that chamomile tea. They say coffee's bad for arthritis, and I don't want what my mother's got, fingers so stiff she can't bend her thumb, and her pen slips off the envelope.

I've been feeling sane these last few minutes. I've met somebody. Truly. I don't mean we're going to bed, just out of the building. I'm ashamed of my map of desires, drawn already, carried always, only waiting for someone to stand still long enough for me to pin my map on their land-scape. Her name is Gloria. We met in a gap in other people's conversa-tions. I saw her navy and red jacket and wondered how she could be so elegant and smiling.

We need somebody busking, I said.

She stopped, looked at my name tag and spoke:

The Minister knew I had the women journos wanting to interview him, he's just announced he's got a plane to catch. I've had no help from the committee, the woman we hired as conference administrator's been working the hours she's been paid for and no more, not that anyone's blaming her, the last thing we want to do is pay a woman part time and expect her to be exploited but one wishes it had been someone prepared to put in a little bit extra. The policy document wasn't ready on time, I've had to explain to everyone on the Board why our Section ought to be op-posing the new legislation, but no-one wants to know about jobs further down the line disappearing if they're going to have a job organising it.

I'm sorry to be going on like this, but I've had just about as much as I can take. The keynote speaker refused to allow her session to be video-taped until the aboriginal delegation had been got down to sit in the front row; now they'll have to be given the floor immediately after lunch. I'm sorry to be going on about it, but I haven't had time to work out what I'm going to say to my own paper; I'm so angry, not just about that, I'm just angry, I don't know who to direct the anger at, and if anybody tells me the photocopier's jammed, I'll ...

Scream, I suggested.

Murder, said Gloria, put her hand on my arm, said she had to check on a few things first, but if she didn't get out in the fresh air for five minutes, murder would be the new item on the agenda. And she disappeared through that orange door.

I shouldn't have lost my last lover. What if I've learned nothing? More than once I've gone out with an umbrella and come home without it. Down at the lost property depot in that old colonnade with winos and pigeon shit under Central Station there are rows of umbrellas. None of them mine. If you could guess the date and destination of the train it was found on you could help yourself to the best umbrella in the world.

I've never got it right. Unfortunately, they know me now. Even if it was my umbrella and I knew the train, carriage and seat, they wouldn't believe me.

There's a woman in a cream suit, with burgundy briefcase. I could dress like that if I had another pair of feet. That's what I want. New feet. It's no good trying to fit the ones I've got into anything fashionable. I can't stand here and radiate cream in these galumphing sneakers. You're good,

125

sneakers, great on a bicycle, but you'd ruin a cream suit.

It's the people with nothing to do that hate this in-between time. Specially as there's something wrong with the air conditioner. There's a woman going through her program for the fourth time. She came here to meet somebody and doesn't want to look up and find out that she hasn't.

If I stood in the middle and announced: All these chairs have to be stacked on that side ready for the next stage of the proceedings, there'd be a stampede.

See that woman. She's grabbed that chair, she's not going to let anyone else carry it. It's a tug-of-war! They're going to pull the legs off. Ooh! She's hitting him over the head with it.

Madam! Let him carry it. People don't want to be mistaken for cardboard. She's hurt him. Quite unnecessarily. There's a man coming over with a red-cross armband and bandages. He looks quite relieved, he's been wanting to help somebody since he got here.

Where is she? Gloria! This time I shall get it right. That's why I keep two mirrors. One for the hairs I have to pull out of my chin, the other to see if I've got the theory right.

1. Financial independence: I swear I won't expect my lover to support me, even if they earn lots of money and I want to be an artist.

2. Emotional independence: No need to swear. Of course I'm self-reliant, grown-up and bullet-proof. If I wasn't, I wouldn't let on.

3. Independence from interference. This is to do with physical impossibilities that a heroine can overcome.

Your relationship must not interfere with your work

Your children must not interfere with your relationship

Your ex must not interfere with your children

Looking after your mother must not interfere with your creativity

Your relationship must not interfere with your friends

The future must not interfere with your relationship

And your relationship must not interfere with talking about it.

That's how I lost my last lover. With two of you trying not to interfere, forget it. It's a law of physics. If you want to be a beam of light, you can't be a particle and wave at the same time.

Gloria's not worrying about lovers. If she had a relationship that broke up, she and her lover would sit down in a Chinese restaurant and work out how to transfer to being good friends — before midnight.

She knows you don't find a lover by looking for one. You work hard, three mornings out of five you take yourself to the heated pool, and there you are, looking into eyes that are looking into yours. Shall we dance?

I haven't danced for years. I mean I haven't been to bed for years. I mean, with somebody. I mean it's only been a few weeks, but every night alone remembers every other night alone, before that and before that, every night forever.

Every night alone a failure because alone.

Every night alone a success because survived alone.

No wonder I'm exhausted. My mother spent the night with him for fifty years.

I know you don't have to have it. You don't have to have shop-bought cappuccino either. Or a radio that gets FM.

I had an aunt who didn't have it. She told me recently, she's very old now, frankly she didn't miss it. She was my father's charity at Christmas. We used to laugh at her.

You can do it yourself. I do do it myself. Round and round. I talk to myself. I also talk to myself. But with two it's a conversation.

Hullo, Gloria.

ALISON LYSSA: I was born with only half a name, Alison. The other half belonged to my father. He was a Member of Parliament with a mission to make sure as many people as possible knew his name. Then they'd vote for him and the world would be saved from the communists, gamblers, unionist, and cheats, who plotted in dank hairy places to destroy democracy and bring young women to ruin. My dad (and my mum) loved to get up somewhere high and make speeches: on the dais opening the Sunday School fete; on the stage at my prize-giving; on the back of the flat-top truck on Saturday morning addressing the shoppers; on the front page of the Sunday papers demonstrating how to break the bus-drivers' strike by joining dad's organised hitch-hike service.

My mother, two sisters and I all had red hair. I think it was a mistake. There was nowhere we could hide.

As soon as I could, I tore down the aisle to swap my dad's name for that of a lovely young man I'd talked into marriage. Nobody asked why I got migraine headaches. A year or two on we had a baby and even the 'Alison' bit of me disappeared entirely when my mother and sister started calling me 'mum'.

Fortunately I had married a thoughtful man. He introduced me to the work of George Eliot, Kate Millet, Betty Friedan and film-maker Peter Watkins (The War Game). When I wrote my own anti-war poem my husband encouraged me, and it was published in Poetry Australia. *My husband introduced me to Gillian Leahy who wore the women's movement badge with the purple fist. I was terrified and fascinated. To find out who we were, my husband and I had to unmarry ourselves and make the rest of our journey apart.*

I needed a name. 'Lyssa' leaped out at me from a dictionary of mythology when Kate Jennings was going to press with the anthology Mother I'm Rooted *and urgently wanted a decision, a name to go with my poems. Kate and I got arrested shortly afterwards, for kissing one another in a marble bar in a city hotel, and I convinced the police, and myself, I was Alison Lyssa. It would lessen the chances of my father finding out I'd been in jail.*

Some years later my dad died. I found in his filing cabinet in a folder named 'Alison', a program for the Nimrod production of my play Pinball, *which is about a lesbian custody case. Pinned to it was his handwritten diatribe against homosexuality.*

'Lyssa' is the Fury of Madness. I felt crazy enough for such a name when I took it on. It was years before I discovered that Lyssa herself wasn't mad. She was commissioned by Hera who had quarrelled with Hercules to send Hercules mad and to drive him out of the city. Stronger than Hercules? I'm working on believing it.

M T C Cronin

You Get Quite a Lot of Stars in a Packet
for Suzie

WHY DID she say that? I was hoping she wouldn't say it. I feel sick. That was exactly what the other one had said. I was really hoping in the back of my mind that she wouldn't mention it. It's unlucky for both of them to say it. I can't say it.

Well, I can actually. But only when I'm alone. I wouldn't say it to anybody. Saying it alone is not really saying it.

I started to wonder whether she'd written it down. She'd given me something in an envelope. It was sealed.

Could I open it?

I didn't think I could — should — open it. I wondered if I should phone anyone. Maybe I could say it over the phone. Maybe I could ring the other one who'd said it and say it to her

No!

I wanted to talk to someone who wouldn't say it. Wouldn't even think of saying it. Would could, have no reason to say it. It's not the sort of thing you'd say for no reason. Which frightened me even more. They'd had a reason. I'd provided them with a reason to say it. I shouldn't have. I'd prompted them to say it. But I hadn't meant to. I wasn't surprised they'd said it but I wasn't expecting them to.

The surprise worried me. I wish I was surprised. But I wasn't.

All that information I'd given them had caused it. Maybe I could take it back. I could make sure I didn't give it to anyone else. But they'd already said it. It would be worse if she'd written it down.

I opened the envelope.

She hadn't.

I didn't feel any better.

Of course she couldn't provide the information. Only I could do that.

I put the envelope in my bag.

*   *   *

I have an appointment, and though an appointment is meant to be for a very particular time and place (and often with a very particular person), my appointment has been changed. This either means that I have a new appointment or that my old appointment has simply been rescheduled.

Moved forward.

As soon as I was advised about this 'moving forward' of my appointment, as if it had been placed on a conveyor belt, I got a parking ticket. Purely because of my moving appointment I cried and stapled the parking ticket to a very personal letter explaining why I could not keep it and mailed it to the person in charge of parking tickets.

Then I rang my friend.

*   *   *

"Hello, hello. I got a parking ticket," I said and started crying, "but I gave it back."

"That's the way," said my friend, "Who do the bastards think they are?"

"They'll probably send it back," I said. "There's probably no process …"

"Take 'em to the High Court," she said. "Six metres from a building alignment simply spells revenue."

I started weeping in a cliched and copious sort of way.

"You seem to be taking it pretty hard," she said, "for someone who's already taken steps."

"It's a long weekend," I blubbered.

*   *   *

Half an hour later she opened my door. She had a key, and a cardboard train with thirteen chocolate eggs in it.

"Which we'll start on right now," she said, "so that we've got somewhere by Sunday."

"I have an appointment," I said, starting to cry again, but not really feeling like it, so stopping. I put down the wine and glasses and unwrapped an egg, which I did feel like.

"And an extremely uninformative way of having a conversation," she said, breaking the cork and two fingernails.

She looked at me as she handed me the bottle. My eyes were on the end of a broom, and went sweep, sweep, sweep around the room.

"Oh well," she said, teeth in an egg, "I imagine there's a whole pile of silly things to find out, if one could be bothered …"

I had an idea, while I was avoiding her and her statements, which were really questions, that I didn't know how the room got arranged like this. Was it planned? Was that vase inevitable, or just green? Had I organised my life in order to have that bookcase exactly right there in the hallway? Was that a premeditated bookcase? I couldn't tell. I squinted at it. Did the books accumulate? Or did they come with it? And what was that chair doing there?

… this room is full of chairs — chairs you can sit in, chairs you can't fill. Do I have a favourite chair? A chair that I cherish above all others? I walked up to one and was about to sit down when I thought … this chair means there's so much you can't do. Try answering the door while you're in this chair, try answering the phone — try cooking up a storm. Try having a shower, having a bath, having a bad day — try to vacuum. You may be able to fuck in this chair — try having someone in the other room.

… and then I heard: "This is a diagnosis, The chair has breast cancer, I'll give it six months to move to the other side of the table. And you! You have to sit in it …"

… chair that I never want to sit in …

… so I turned on it — what the fuck are you doing chair? Chair what do you do? Arsehold chair, cunt chair, dumb-as-a-fish chair …

"Did you know that chairs hold people — other things just sit on them …" I could barely hear my own voice in the room.

"Please sit down."

"Please sit down," I heard again. "Come on, are you O.K?" The chair was talking.

"The room has grown around me," I whispered back.

"Just sit down," she said, putting a glass in my hand.

So I sat down. The chair looked good and I had no absolute or free will left. Who was it who said, *"it is never we who affirm or deny something of a thing, but it is the thing itself that affirms or denies, in us, something of itself. We don't desire a thing because we judge it to be good but rather we judge it to be good because we desire it."* Me and the chair desired each other — so I sat …

"I have an appointment," I said.

"So you said," she said.

I noticed there were nine eggs left on the train. "I went to see someone and she sent me to see someone else and now I have to go and see someone else," I blurted, "and it runs in the family."

"First time I ever heard of going to see someone running in the family," she said, "but then again, you're a pretty gregarious mob."

"Yes," I went on, "and he's gone away for Easter, with my breast — or at least the thought it — in his hands."

"Hopefully, he won't take off his rubber gloves all weekend," she said.

"And he said, it will only be a few days, but that's a lifetime — at least to go without a breast and I am trying to pretend but all I can think is I hope it's having a good time … Gee, I wouldn't mind getting away for Easter …" I ran out of breath and drank some wine and peeled another egg from a pink shiny wrapper. There were only six left.

"I think I finally get the picture," she said. "My surgeon took my breast on a skiing holiday to Switzerland. By the time he got back it was frozen solid and he had to operate on the Ice Maiden." She took off her shirt and showed me a scar on a breast.

"These aren't just words," she said, pointing with her finger to the scar someone else had made, "but our ways of jumping skin. Now, if you can go to the shop and get these things …" she jumped up and made a list near the phone, "… I'll cook you a wonderful dinner and we'll talk all night."

*   *   *

When I got back, my friend had run the bath, put some candles on the toilet seat, turned off the light and said "Get in!"

I lay in the bath and watched bits of me float. One breast lolling, like the tongue of a dog. The other … gone to the dogs? Who knows? I stared up at the ceiling, but it wasn't there … It had become a sky. A universe of tiny stars twinkled from out of the darkness. I felt like dreaming and crying and even having a sense of humour again. I could smell garlic and hear the voice of someone with a beautiful scar singing. I stared up at the ceiling-sky. It occurred to me that you get quite a lot of stars in a packet. I laughed and wondered if the place where she'd bought them sold packets of boobs …

I yelled out, "Hey, are there any chocolate eggs left?"

M.T.C. CRONIN is often a poet — she has written a novel consisting of 144 separate poems, entitled Hate of the Dead — sometimes a writer of fiction — is working at present on a prose novel — occasionally the author of short stories — viz — and under duress, the thrower-together of lyrics for a band of friendly and persuasive musicians.

She grew up in Caloundra Qld — most of the time, and precisely, in a place called Currimundi Lake — and now lives in Sydney (the result of a love affair).

She has travelled extensively, sleeps a lot, drinks a lot and eats a lot, is extremely argumentative, prone to fear and panic, but is quite prepared to have a good time if at all possible.

She is currently in her third year of the MA (Writing) at the University of Technology, Sydney, and adores her cats but can't pay her vet bill because the little bastards keep getting into trouble. It's a busy road. A doberman wanders the streets at night and it only takes one bark to have her on the footpath at four in the morning calling: puss, puss, puss …

At the moment she is tired.

FINOLA MOORHEAD

Cressida,
a prose poem of dog-maidens

1

This retreat I contemplate is no retreat from the battle (one of many in what war). The distraction hits like a blast of Westerly wind arriving to rattle loose windows
and be here wholly — distracting.

So it is with English, the one word is its opposite, neither really naming the intention. Perhaps the distraction names it better, angling sounds through the leaves, being the motion and attitude, being the way of the leaves then — that is, now, the moment.

But it travels and one hears it farther off, behind, in front, elsewhere — coming, being. Retreat and presence, gusts of wind from the deserts of Eastern Australia's sunset, gathering restless strength slipping to and from on the barometer.

Such is retreat,
barometric withdrawal.
I am no longer a part
of the game which hasn't
been played on a
fair, square platform.
I leave my puff and gusts
and disappear,
your lies of me
in your pocket
burning holes
like smoking guns
telling tales.

2

I cannot bear to see your blush although my agency might force you to it;
your humiliation is also mine.
I let you have it.

Again English turns tables, but you can have it. I am leaving by being here.

Should the battle, though, whip up arriving at the shattering glass, then, also, I will let you have it, as now I stay gathering strength, marshalling forces in strained solitude or
ordered retreat.

Provided with provisions, lop-sided with provisions. Again the language attacks me with multiple meanings. Yet I ask nothing of the worded paper, the blunt pencil. It is just that I have the time for it and the wind distracts me.

The battle rages like the winds in distant hills signifying presence.

3

Why did the little lantern smoke and hiss as if to explode? While I, in some memory, hear the moaning of Cressida, meaningless rhymes occur to me: who married Thetis to the sea?

Through the trees a second of light, two times flashing, as a car grinds revving up the hill begging recognition, welcome possibly, and the slim moon now follows the sun into the mauve West
nether. Idle curiosity asks: who goes past the gate?

Not Cressida, for who is she? She, not Charon, calls for my pennies, my price, as she mourns across some distant age. Count the years in hundreds of thousands, not four, not forty — too long, even the rocks have forgotten. The rock herself is silent. No, says this stranger, Cressida, she is not dumb, nor deaf, not dense nor fossilised,
she hears.

Cressida takes up the cadence and we hear the moans of the rock and we interpret her moans, she mourns.

She mourns lost heavens.
She calls her daughter, Perdita.
· She rests on the mattress on my verandah and she stares sullenly from her portrait. Even so, I ask her for the poem, not her poem,
my poem.

And, kind as women are, she obliges and leaves me swaying between

134

Lethe and Mnemosthene, forgetting and remembering in one restless windy action. Zephyrous request: Who walked on my grave? Who, so careless of the goddess, dances on the sacred rocks with cloven hoof and hobbed nail crushing the air out of the song? And knowing that she, he, they do, why do they make such a racket, afterwards? Is it perhaps to drown the strange cries of Cressida, the weeping vehicle of the silent rock?

4

Now the language
like wind suddenly absent
stirs me up,
makes me play its game
to the final gambit.
What poem, what is poem
and who dares poetry
with this crude, unwieldy tool,
English.
The rock does not know
English
and English has no word
pure enough
for the hard dirt
that holds us firm
with gravity to her breast.
Earth, you might say,
but you say the least of it,
for it includes the ghostly tombstone
of the moon,
the dark barks of dogs in the night
and twinkling Venus,
impersonal coo-ees echoing
presence —
a coming —
a becoming.
A welcome maybe.
Here, sit, let me listen to you.
Talk woman.
Then you, too, drown
the whine with your whinge,
the waterfall with your tears,
the distant distress of Cressida

with your sobs.
I can handle your sorrow,
it's mundane,
like mine. You'll live,
coo-ee, dog bark,
footsteps of the huntress
heard, for the horse is heavy.

Dog maidens abound in these hills
and now the moon is set, they
carry torches with batteries,
or torches of tin-cans and petrol candles,
or kerosene lanterns, like mine.
I will sit and listen,
but you must come to me
and know to whom you are coming
for I am in retreat,
my back is turned,
you will have to catch my attention
and want it, then I will attend you.

5

Listen. Shush. Hush. Irish stew bubbling with heat. The fire moves the
molecules of the food with the water and the tastes of carrot and parsley,
lamb and flour, onion, potato, pepper combining edibly ...
while the poem lets it stick to the base of the clay pot.
I attend to it with water and wooden spoon and think of the lie, Thetis.
Of the sea, he was she. Cressida and I recall that battle.

It raged for an age and was won by sleight of hand, a simple trick, cards
up the sleeve. Bland, cynical faces relying on secrecy for their serenity
which we inferred was a spiritual power we had not yet heard of, for we
never held that the devil you know is better than the one you don't. The
next we always thought could be another goddess. By that time we were
eager for change; a revolution never hurt anyone, we thought.
We were fools.

We were fooled and we lost our naming. Thetis of the sea became he and
trickery and chicanery did it. For a thousand years we watched in-
credulous, open-mouthed, stunned, mermaids aghast like mullet on the
rocks, lost — Perdita.

6

Daughter, Perdita, how could you carry that name and not blame your
mother for her perfidy?
Yet it is true, my daughter, you are lost, as we all became lost, in different
generations, like single cells.
Perdita daughter,
Hilda, Emma, Roberta mother.
Jane, Jenny, Juanita crone.

They were crows, the old crones.
Nothing would please them, bitter of mouth,
bitter of tongue. If you danced in your tutu
in front of them, for them, on magic legs
of mermaids that sliced through your abdomen,
their lips tightened like misers' purses and they
squawked together in disapproval. Your tears
did not move them. There's nothing sweet
about a crone. Hags they were, death-dealers
and crude, filthy-minded bitter old bitches,
the crones. Resenting us who were forever young.
They could not forgive our stupidity, our frivolity,
our lack of foresight. Gloom, doom, they foretold,
and gloom and doom came. Still they weren't satisfied.
It was their youth, their stolen youthhoods
they wanted redressed. But it was gone,
and gradually they lost their wisdom too.
Leaving us to be raped and reborn, raped and reborn,
ravaged beyond our womanspeak.
We could not remember the words, nor the signs
for the words or even, after some time,
the wordless significance. Men's voices saturated
the fine tunes in the rock heart and the thunder of hooves
battered the vibrations of the earth down to such a low decibel
it took a hundred years for a single sound wave
to break on the shore of a sentient ear — Perdita,
daughter, deaf as a post
like the gummy old crones around their pots,
laughing at crudities and munching soft meat,
spitting out seeds with disgust.

7

Cloud rises with the dawn, stillness as well, after a night of wind banging windows and rattling locks like playful spooks, ghosts retelling in gusts the great war of mythology in my waking moments.

Dreams stay like fossils
in the ground
sketching patterns on the silence.
Leave them be.

Glorify your crones if you must, and see, too, if you can make English tell your tale of anguish. If you can call out the anachronism, Woe, and be believed, then do it.

Try it. He will hear you in the safety of his own language wherein the sickle of the old rock has no cut, rather descends innocently, scientifically, following the sun below the North-Western hill. When, in fact, it is Amaltheia's blade on her way to cut old Kronos' balls off, on her way to slice the sack, to watch the spermy blood drop on Rhea's skull. She wants to see what Rhea will do: will she rage or comply with growth and birth and rebirth? His language has no notion of the real battle as goddess with goddess lock antlers and fish-tails. All he can see is the horn of plenty, Cornucopia, full of the fruits of early winter. And he, the Old Goat, sees himself as the God of Fertility.

His is the language you speak
when you say,
    Woe is I,
    Woe is me,
Woe is the earth. You play your play to males, well each he will chuckle there and say yeah yeah, that is what we want, sorrowing witches and toothless crones, deaf, lost daughters. You gave me your humiliation and our inadequacy, sure result of rape and ravage, it is his victory. As you and she prance out your ignorance, it is the pain he loves in the mermaids' dance.

She, who would never burn the pot and likes my Irish stew with dumplings in it, did not ask for this poem. Yet, I reheat the brew within the rhythms and the hidden rhymes as the winds have brought a clear day in and it's lunchtime. The battle lies dormant, sleeping in the overhead sun, strolling through the grasses with the odd chirp and buzz of small life, blow-fly and bird with yellow breast and black helmet, but the game is not over.

8

So speak, sister,
calling snake cousin,
serpent mother-in-lore,
speak with your tongue
resting behind closed lips.
Speak in the action of listening,
fool, like me.

So you talk to your dog
I talk to my asses' ears
but do we hear, sister?
Do we hear the vegetable grow
or notice the excitement
with which she brings forth her first flower
or care for her worry
about the fate of the fruit to come?
Or do we vegetate?
There the clashing irony of English
blasts lies like heavy metal percussion
in our ears in rhythms no more subtle
than the heart-beats in the breasts of men:
take that
take that
and that.
Slap, stomp and groan.
Scream in the house music
of domestic violence
with images worn thin
even for him and
repeated ad infinitum.

9

They come in throbbing Holdens, sirens of the double struggle, to nail
witchhunt messages on the gate. I twist my head like a questioning collie
and wonder at the vulgar lines: am I next for the treatment, mad daugh-
ters?
I know why I've drawn the fire
I see the joke but I cannot laugh
I feel the stab but it does not hurt.
Have you joined forces?
Or is it a single shot out of the distant battle which has dogged my life,

across the sea, the mountains and the sky?

Sodden poet in rain-dark forest, it was the wind that loosed the courage to recite and declaim like a busker in the Devonshire Street tunnel, so brash and loud the sacred words; sodden poet in rain-dark corridor, playing the fool to clever fools, so money fell into the hat on the floor and belonged then to none of us and burnt in the fire, a second of flame. I, sodden now, grasp for a modicum of confidence, as during the day I scrape a sculpture out of firewood, a totem sea-horse with wings. A present. Thus I am strung between value and value and have to choose or cringe as any other brown-nose sleazing to be pleasing, knowing that praise like the currency note lasts half a moment in the heat. Okay I'll bear my fear alone and wear this pencil down to a stub.

Too much like getting nowhere
tying women not meaning in knots
is not retreat with a straight back.

10
The slandering faces
leave the streets
to ply their sibilant
tongues in the bush,
to undermine the fragile power
of compassion for each other.

As women meet, clumsily communicating in the language of opposites, English, German, babble, where bubble probably means pin, the raging quietude frustrates as it erupts into dance without ritual or mirth at the lame joke. Each woman goes with a heavy heart to find a sign on her gate making fun of her precisely at the point of her utmost vulnerability. She cannot understand the battle's proximity nor why the smoking gun is in the fist of a friend.

The energy drains out of her like menopausal blood
and bones ache at the marrow with the onset of age.
She does not lie to sleep with dreams of the future
for the future has no images for her but the hope
that the lines called crows' feet are creases of beauty,
etching of a life where fights
taken up were for justice and truth, sympathy and humour.

Even so who will take the time
to notice such subtle delineation?
Who will pick the wise crone
from the crowd of toothless hags
still bitching at each other in their cowardice?
That mob in glistening black plumage
point arthritic claws at the healer
among them and cry, it is she who brings sickness!

Indeed
it is why
they feared
the Goddess.
She ruled
birth growth
death and
desolation,
each a certainty
as is disease.

11

When the crusaders came back from the Holy Land they brought with them
knowledge of the wasteland. They had seen the desert, those terrifying
sandhills of the Sahara and Middle East, which once, in the living memory
of a few centuries were rooted down and fertile. It was green when the
goddess was honoured. Grain grew there in the seasons of the moon and
the harvest festivals worshipped the Holy Female for the plenty, orgies
were celebrations and release of tension, a dance in the body, a mud lark
of smut, rejoicing that she who gave could also take away and the cycle
would continue. The heaven and hell of crusading christendom born out
of fear of the shifting sandhills, the thirsty wastelands of Allah who had
swallowed woman, were the politics of scare tactics.
Do not frighten me, agents of disaster, realists hugging the decreasing
flood plains of the Nile and other rivers, you who know that everyone
cannot live there, territorialists marking boundaries with piss and barbed
wire fences and the threatening gestures that power over is power per se.

We whip up a cauldron and the witches flee,
the swirling winds being too much for us.
We cannot contain the past and future in our meagre present.
It is better to natter knives in the back than stand akimbo with weapons

displayed.

For there were patriarchal wars, bigger than Peloponnesian, the Great War, Vietnam or Civil wars over that Semitic desert put together, and in these wars witches, hags, sirens, mermaids, virgins, mothers, whores and crones took up arms beside the amazons in defence of the Goddess. To be defeated, as it happened, colonised, humiliated and eventually turned over to slavery. Sexual slavery is the practice of Goddess annihilation and women today exist with little more than a disappearing chimera of her own divinity, Fata Morgana.

Fata Morgana, a mirage over the desert, tantalisingly fluid and un-approachable, is unreal or unrealised by the realists who do not want to understand. Comprehension is the least of their needs as they squabble over squares of sand, those grids of land pegged out on maps of ownership by the surveys of invasion.

Realist women, if you want to wear purdah and be stoned for your own rape, come with your sibilant slander, come to the forests where dog maidens roam, carrying bags, come with your English and scream abuse, destroy some more, for that is what you do. Stupid daughters of stupefied mothers and youthless crones, why do you turn on the goddess in each other? You cannot test her strength that way. She can die like the earth.

Is it because you don't believe?
Your distrust comes from your ignorance oh arrogant girls of the Lesbian generation.

Don't blame alone the paucity of the language we inherit, we need more understanding than that, more compassion and humour than that, my sisters.

12
Does the tree love the axe,
the grass the blade? For I know
the masochist loves the sadist —
I've been told.

Sometimes it's hard to make one's way through the forest of women's lies because half the time they're there to enable them simply to survive. And they come in such variety, youth, childhood, psychology, blood hardly

142

explain: why does it matter to women so much to be liked, to have their moral courage stripped from them like a blouse, preventing rape by saying okay, and lying, doing it willingly?

Fear, fear, fear of fear to be fearing.
The helicopters shatter the soundscape
and scatter the women scuttling under brush
and bush and lantana, ducking away from sight
in army greens — condition terrorised —
shaking in company with obsessed monologues.

Feral in the wilderness
and violent are the times
when clean souls are mirrors
of monstrous psychology,
thus hunted as beasts
as bad as razorbacks.
Seeking refuge,
seeking asylum,
like plague victims
in a bomb shelter,
they turn on each other,
scratching, kicking, slandering,
crying blindly.

The poem, inadequate in language grasps nerve ends like wisps of cigarette smoke, finds in its palm nothing but air, holds its place on the waves no more than a rolling moment and knows not where to go or whether indeed it has been. The rain beats down the wind in the months to come and no sculpture of firewood healed the wounds of difference, bleeding hearts in the rain forest dripping pungent on the mulch screeched like fighting black cockatoos flashing red tails, flashing red angry lights from their third eyes, distressed, for women see.

When respect dies and sense of wonder
lies down face down tied thrashing
in the bondage of psychology,
threads of darkened spirituality escape
and coil up like fork-tongued snakes
spitting in fear-provoked aggression,
poised for attack, to slay the dragons ...
in the mirror

congregating in the mirror
trembling on the surface of the mirror
illusions of fire and smoke from mouth and nostril
their own reflection in the souls of the pure.

Lay assault on the light, put out the lights
that ugly fluorescence shows too much, truth.

13
Then the mirrors turned on me
everywhere I looked my own failure
disgusted me. The forest of females
was a prism of reflecting glass,
catching fire, burning fear.

Or fear lighted by the sun caught
in a magnifying lens addressing
the subject-matter me took flame
and the blush heated my cheeks
as I saw my own haunted stare.

I had nothing to say that could help
deaf ears and tear-blinded eyes,
no springs bubbling out of the earth here
in my soul to water the flames
and no escape routes, no escapism.

Everything betrayed me to myself.
It was as if I feared the dogs myself
and saw the dragons in myself
testing the goddess of myself
in my own violence with myself.

Cressida calls from a long dark night,
so far away, so faint in the dreamscape,
the soft thud of her wave upon my shore
registers in the confusion of the subconscious
Which I can hardly recall as I wake ...

Wake too slowly, too shakily, to the realisation
that my criticism of women must come
back on me making me know my faults are

not projections of others' fears on my mirror
but my own somehow as theirs are theirs.

Finola Moorhead: Fell in love with my first woman several days after my first period and spent the ghastly years of my adolescence swinging between confusion and exhilaration, disgust and purity. At a Catholic boarding school, I was sent down with my bedding to a junior dormitory as a punishment of my openly ad-mitted lesbian feelings. That was ok. I had the feelings anyway, the trial by older girls and the authorities was something else to be dealt with.

It happened again in my early university days. They sent me to Coventry for a few months for a lesbianism I wasn't even practising at the time. Shrug. I'd taken the rap for others ever since I can remember. I, rather, romanticised my difference into the notion of being (becoming) a writer, wrote soul-felt poetry in the midnights of black coffee on foolscap over unread texts and tried to figure out the heterosexual world. I was at university when the first demonstrations against the Vietnam War happened and enjoyed an extracurricular education there. Then I taught for four years in a couple of country schools. While doing that I wrote my first plays and got accepted as one of the playwrights to be helped in the first Australian National Playwrights Conference. That was all my ambition needed.

Thenceforth I was a writer and went to the Adelaide Festival's Writers' Week and met writers. Older writers, women writers, avant garde writers and es-tablished correspondences on the subject of writing. I managed to get a couple of fellowships during the Whitlam years. I worked as a reader for Meanjin quarterly, poring over others' unpublished writing, making decisions as to its worth — myself and AA Phillips. I guess that sharpened my critical faculty and con-fidence.

In the middle 70's I became a feminist lesbian writer and worked with the Women's Theatre Group in Melbourne until it folded. I travelled and came back and got a Writer-in-residency at Monash University at which place I began work on Remember the Tarantella. *In 1985 my first two books came out,* A Hand-written Classic *and* Quilt, *a selection of prose. After the publication of the novel, experiencing suppression of that work, I found myself in the Supreme Court of New South Wales stating that I was a radical lesbian separatist, proudly.* Still Murder, *which won the Vance Palmer Fiction Prize in 1991, was written while I was receiving money from the Literature Board of the Australia Council.*

Now I am working on a third novel which will make a trilogy with the pre-vious two and will take my notion of lesbian power a little deeper, a little further. I expect it will take me a few years to complete.

CATHERINE BATESON

Swimmers

WE SWIM face to face, a swimmer and her double, her pacer. It is impossible to tell us apart — goggles turn us into exotic insects — we are all movement and open mouths. Watch — we swim face to face, both heads turning the same second, barely skimming the water's surface, to gulp sweet air. Our arms lift, pull through the water, pull us through the water.

You stand at the mirror, hair thrown forward to be towelled dry. I watch you, watch me. Our movements are reflected in the other's tensed arms as hair is dried and brushed. We could be Degas women, forever raising plump arms as we untangle strands of knotted hair. But there is no artist at this keyhole, just you and I. You watch me/watch you.

Two women, the same height, the same build. When we swim together we are two swimmers, doubles. Each keeps the other's speed.

You stand at the mirror. Your hands, which now hold the towel to me, are my hands — the same broad palms, the same long fingers. With that gesture we are linked — enclosed in the space of a movement from you to me.

This movement — a dialogue. The silence wraps us surely, making us sisters, lovers. There are identical lines under our eyes from the goggles. We smile — the towel is a suspended bridge.

We swim into the night. Under each other's hands, breath is quickened, sharpened until each breath is a razor drawn across the night's surface. We cut the night into streamers. Beached back on land you ask, is this power? Power? Is that your word for this — this rising to meet each other, firework flowering, slow-motion explosion through water up to the air as we merge before splitting — strange atom, not to ruin but to dis/fuse — two made one, made separate?

If this is power — your head thrown back in answer to my fingers, my tongue … I don't know, I reply.

Outside it rains. The roads are seal-slick and shiny. Your fingers tattoo patterns into my flesh — here bright as lightning, there like thunder.

Downstairs, in a bowl of fresh water, a saltwater stone, picked up on sand, shatters quietly.

On the first floor I fragment.

Return.

I say, I knew a poet once who only wrote at 2 am. She claimed quality of tiredness allowed her ... you are asleep. I examine your hand which burrows between my breasts. It is, as I knew, my hand, variations. It is after midnight. I go downstairs. A cat cries to be let in, out of the rain which is steadily drenching the night. I reassemble the broken stone. I can see myself reflected in the window.

I am you/me/she.

CATHERINE BATESON: This piece was a hesitant starting point for an exploration of prose/poetry and small prose pieces which do not so much tell a story as reflect a mood or emotion. At the time I was reading writers such as Helene Cixous, Luce Irigaray, Nicole Brossard, Betsy Warland and Daphne Marlatt.

FLIGHT OF KOALAS
Margaret Bradstock

This is a book about journeys, especially the journeys women make today — with all the baggage of desire, the need for knowledge, love and freedom. The poems take flight to various places: Europe, South-East Asia, the 500 bus route in Sydney, the Blue Mountains, and finally an impressive sequence about travelling in China. They explore the relationships between mother and daughter, the tragedy of AIDS, the difficult paths of feminism, the births and deaths of ordinary people.

'terse, immediate and keenly observant' —Judith Beveridge
'thoughful, provocative, observant' — Aust Book Review
'Strong poems, fine perceptions' —Judith Rodriguez

Recommended Retail $ 9.95   ISBN 1 875243 10 0

BlackWattle Press

Available from good bookshops everywhere, just ask
or write to PO Box 4, Leichhardt NSW 2040 (incl $2 postage)